MW00439411

MURDER LIVE

A Highland Springs suspense novel, Book 1

By Cynthia Hickey

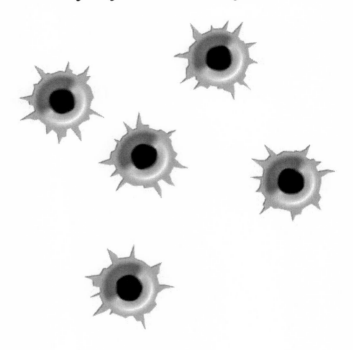

ISBN-13: 978-1-946939-30-2
ISBN-10: 1-946939-30-7

DEDICATION

Dedication: For my readers who love an edge-of-your seat thriller.

Dedication: For my readers who love an edge-of-your seat thriller

CHAPTER ONE

She wasn't his first kill. In fact, she was his tenth. That meant he needed a cool serial killer name. Something that glorified the man who planned on terrorizing Highland Springs, the Podunk town his birth mother dropped him in and abandoned him when he could barely walk then reentered his life later on, convinced he would forgive and forget. The cozy town nestled in the Ozarks had never risen to the standards of a man with his intelligence.

He twisted his lips and stared into the wide eyes of the bound and gagged. "What do you think I should be called?"

She squealed in response, the gag preventing any noise of real value. No one would hear her scream. He would silence her forever except for the screams caught in cyberspace for eternity.

Ah, yes. "The Silencer. Thank you." He patted her cheek too hard to be a love tap and positioned her cell phone into the holder on the tripod. No more would his deeds go unnoticed. From now on, they'd be posted live for all his victim's family and friends to see. Why should he be the only one to have all the fun?

Once the camera was ready and recording, he pulled on a ski mask, grabbed a knife, and pressed the button on an old-fashioned tape player. The lyrics to the "Mockingbird" song began to play. "Hush little baby, don't say a word…"

Sharlene Camenetti pulled her hair back into a ponytail, made sure her badge was straight and headed out the front door. "Going to work now, Candy!"

"Bye, Shar." Her sister-slash-roommate thrust a piece of buttered toast into her hand. "What have I told you about skipping breakfast?"

"I'm grabbing a bagel at The Brew." Shar grinned and slapped the screen door so it banged against the house. Her way of saying goodbye and driving her sister nuts. She slid into the driver's seat and headed for the coffee shop. If she arrived at their tiny police station without bagels and coffee in hand, there would be a mutiny of two—her deputy and her receptionist.

A bell jingled over the door of The Brew. A young woman with purple hair and multiple tattoos glanced up from behind the counter. "Mornin', Sheriff."

"Mornin', Susy. I'll have the usual. Don't skimp on the cream cheese." She placed a twenty-dollar bill on the counter.

The honk of a horn and the sound of breaking glass drew Shar's attention to the plate-glass window in time to see a truck of teenage boys bat a side-view mirror off a Cadillac. "What the…hold my coffee!" She dashed out the door and thundered down the sidewalk. When the truck stopped at a red light, Shar yanked open the passenger door and dragged the hoodlum out.

"Mason Monroe. Wait until your father hears about this." Shar pushed him against the side of the rusty Ford. "Bobby, you might as well get out and join us.

You don't even have a driver's license. You know better than to let someone without a license drive your vehicle, Mason. Whoever is hiding under that blanket in the back had better come on out, too. Don't make me shoot you."

"You wouldn't." Mason scowled and stomped to the sidewalk as his friends joined him. "That's police brutality."

"Maybe I won't shoot you, but you sure make me want to, and you have no idea what police brutality is." She crossed her arms and shook her head. "Explain yourselves."

They all started talking at once.

"Bobby, you're the driver, you talk." Shar speared the boy with a sharp glance.

"There's nothing to do in this Podunk town." He kicked at a rock in the road.

"So you were bored?" Shar frowned. "This is going to cost your folks a pretty penny because I can see you did this all the way up Main Street. Park that heap of a truck over there and join us at the coffee shop."

"We get coffee?" Mason straightened up.

"I get coffee. You get put in holding until your parents come and get you. Move it." She waved them in front of her. "Don't be stupid and try to run, Bobby Miller. I know where you live, and I'll be mighty pissed when I come fetch you."

She made the boys stand against the window while she picked up her purchase, then crammed all five of them into the backseat of her jeep. Not conventional, but safer than what they were causing havoc in.

At the station, she handed the bag of bagels to her receptionist, Amber, shook her head at the way the boys ogled the young woman's cleavage, then shoved Mason toward holding. "Put your tongue back in your mouth, scamp, and move. Come on, the rest of you, too. There's a phone for you to call home. If I find one mark of graffiti, I'll arrest you in addition to getting you in trouble with your mom and dad."

Shar saw no reason to babysit the boys since the door could and windows could only be opened from the outside and was in full view of her office through the large glass windows. She sat at her desk and propped her feet up. She slathered a thick layer of strawberry cream cheese on a plain bagel, toasted the boys with her coffee, and sat back to wait.

By the time she finished her breakfast, Mark Mayfield, her very own Barney Fife, led five pairs of red-faced parents into her office. They all squeezed inside and demanded to know why she was picking on their little angels.

When they'd finished ranting, she informed them of the multiple calls to the reception desk and how she'd witnessed them with her own eyes destroying a mirror on Mrs. Gladstone's caddy.

Once they'd redirected their anger from Shar to their offspring, Shar stood. "I'm more than happy to release the boys into your capable hands. As long as restitution is made to the owners of the affected vehicles, we'll let the matter go. No sense in hurting these boys' chances of getting into a good college." Not that one of them had a lick of sense in their heads.

Mr. Monroe, high school football coach, bobbed Mason in the back of the head the moment the boy was free. "Six months of yard work! I don't care if it's hot or cold. I ought to take you off first-string quarterback and put you on third." He grabbed his son by the arm and dragged him from the building, the missus trailing behind.

"What a way to start the day." Mark grinned, his round face beaming. "Don't you love small town life?"

"Yes, Mark, I do." Shar moved to the reception desk where Amber was filing her ridiculously long nails. "Any messages?"

She popped a bubble. "Yep. You got those complaints you told the parents about. You sure do know people, Sheriff."

"It's my job. What else?"

Her smile faded. "I'm not sure, but a girl from the Dairy Queen said her friend never met her this morning."

"How long ago was this?"

"She was supposed to meet up with her two hours ago."

"At six a.m.?" They couldn't have been up to any good. Mason and his buddies were right. There wasn't a whole lot to do in Highland Springs other than eating ice cream, swimming, and making out. Unless you had a car and money in your pocket. Then you could drive the hour to Eureka Springs. Shar took the information and headed back to her office. "Mark, go speak with the friend while I call the parents."

As soon as Shar settled behind her desk, she dialed the number on the message. "Mrs. Holston? This is Sheriff Camenetti. A..." she glanced at the message, "Maggie said your daughter, Rachel, was supposed to meet her at six a.m. this morning, but never arrived. Is she home?"

"No, she told us she spent the night with a friend.

Harold!" The woman's shriek rang through the phone.

Shar held the receiver away from her ear while the woman frantically told Harold about Maggie not being where she said she was going to be. Several minutes later, she got back on the phone. "We're on our way to see you." Click.

Well, okay. Shar hung up the phone and wrote down the names. When Mark returned, they could compare notes and see whether they had cause for concern. It wouldn't be the first time an unhappy teen ran away from home and reappeared a few days later hungry and tired.

The clicking of Amber's heels on the tile, followed by the more muffled sounds of soft-soled shoes, alerted Shar to the fact that the Holstons had arrived. She stood and took a deep breath. These were her people. A couple of the voters responsible for her being sheriff. She could do this. She could satisfy them.

"Mr. and Mrs. Holston, please have a seat." She waved a hand to the two chairs in front of her desk. "Amber, water please."

"We've tried calling her cell phone," Mrs. Holston said, "but it goes straight to voice mail."

"May I have it, please." She held out her hand for the phone, then pressed a button on her receiver and called Mark. "Step into my office, please."

He was there in seconds. "Yes?"

"See if you can put a trace on this. If the phone is on, we'll be able to track it." She forced a smile. "Did you have an argument last night?" She turned back to the parents.

"No." The father shook his head. "Rachel was a bit of a free-spirit, stubborn, but we rarely fought. We'd had dinner together the night before." He raised his red-rimmed eyes to Shar's. "This is unlike her, Sheriff."

Shar met his gaze for several minutes. "We'll find her. I'll do everything in my power."

By the end of the day, she was tired, hungry, and wanting nothing more than to sit in front of the television with a glass of wine—make that two—and a bowl of buttered popcorn. Unfortunately, Candy had other ideas.

"You promised you'd go out to dinner with me." She glared. "What's the point of living together if we never hang out?"

"Fine." Shar slammed her bedroom door and changed her clothes.

FBI agent, Everis Hayes, checked into the one and only motel in Highland Springs, Arkansas, set his briefcase on the green and yellow bedspread, then plugged in his laptop. He pulled up the post of interest and swallowed against the mountain in his throat.

He couldn't be one hundred percent positive without seeing the man's face, but his gut told him the man on the film was none other than the killer he'd been hunting the past two years. A man who had killed ten women over the course of those two years. This was the first time he'd recorded the action, but it had to be him.

Loosening his tie, he pulled it off and tossed it on his bed. Nothing sounded better at that moment than a long hot shower. He pressed his fingers on the bed. A more comfortable mattress might be good. He groaned and headed for the bathroom, not relishing what could be an unpleasant visit to the local sheriff in the morning.

With the water as hot as he could bear, Everis stepped under the spray. He lay one palm flat against the tile and closed his eyes. What if coming here was a waste of time? What if the man in the video—while a killer—wasn't the man he'd been chasing? He slapped the tile. If he was right, Highland Springs was about to see more evil than they were ready for.

His stomach protested, not having eaten since breakfast, which spurred Everis into pulling on a pair of jeans and a clean black tee shirt. He combed his wet hair back, trying his best to smooth out the curls. Failing, he slapped on a baseball cap and headed for the barbecue joint next door.

Country music blared through the swinging doors. Everis made a beeline for the bar, ordered a beer and wings, then turned to survey the room. His attention immediately concentrated on a pair of beauties. While the brunette was quite pretty, the raven-haired beauty was a vision in tight jeans, red boots, and black spaghetti strap top that showed off her curves. He grinned, then winked as they cast glances his way.

If he weren't in town on a case, he'd definitely pursue his possibilities. He tapped the rim of his cap and grabbed his beer before heading to a table in the corner where he had a clear view of all entrances to the restaurant.

Wouldn't it be nice if the killer waltzed in and announced himself?

CHAPTER TWO

Shar plugged in her laptop and went straight to Rachel Holston's Facebook page. Today's young seemed to think the world wanted to know every bit of their business. There it was. Her announcement to everyone that she was meeting Maggie at the DQ. What followed next froze the blood in Shar's veins.

She watched in horror as a masked man cut out the living girl's tongue and tossed it at the camera. He then took the same knife and slit her throat.

Wiping the weapon on his black pants, he looked straight at the camera. "I'm The Silencer. We'll meet again." Fade to black.

"What kind of madman kills a young girl and posts it on her Facebook page?" Shar took a sip of her coffee to wash the sour taste of fear and disgust from her mouth.

"The kind I've been chasing for two years." The handsome dark-haired man she'd spotted at the restaurant last night strode into her office and offered his hand. "Everis Hayes, Arkansas Bureau of Investigation."

"Sheriff Camenetti." Shar returned his shake, doing her best to ignore the jolt of electricity that shot up her arm at the contact, and motioned for him to sit in the chair across from her. "You know this guy?"

"Know of him. No idea who he is." Agent Hayes leaned back in the chair, propping his feet on the corner of her battered metal desk. "This is the first time he's filmed his killing. Or cut out the victim's tongue, come to think of it."

"He acted as if he was playing some kind of sick game." Shar pressed a button on her phone. "Amber, bring our visitor a cup of coffee, please."

"Much obliged."

Shar gave a thin-lipped smile. "What can I do for you, Agent Hayes?"

"Work with me." His grin dazzled the sun. "I'm new to the Arkansas and Ozark area, having come from Philadelphia. I bet you know everything about everyone around here, and you also know your way around."

"That I do." She crossed her arms and studied him. He looked like a fed in his dark suit and shiny cowboy boots. If her gut was right, he'd have some scuffs on his boots before this case was finished. "Not a lot goes on around here, Agent. This is probably the worst in over twenty years. While I'm grateful for, and accept your help, don't think for a minute that I'm not capable of doing my job."

"I wouldn't dare." He grinned again, taking his boots off her desk as Amber entered the room. "I checked up on you before coming. You seem quite capable, and the people of this town think highly of you."

"Here you go, sir." Amber leaned over in her tight knitted dress and set a mug of black coffee on the desk. She placed a packet of sugar and cream next to it and tossed him a flirtatious glance. "Anything else?"

"That's it, thank you." He chuckled and cast an

amused look at Shar.

Surprising. Most men reveled in Amber's attention. Respect for the man rose a notch. "That will be all, Amber."

Pouting, the receptionist sashayed from the room.

"We found a body we believe to be Rachel Holston." Mark rushed into the room. "Someone dumped it out by Cedar Creek. Hikers found it." Face pale, he shook his head.

Shar stood and grabbed her holster and jacket. "You're welcome to ride with me, Agent. Deputy Mayfield, meet Federal Agent Hayes. He's here to help us catch this creep." She raced out the door to her jeep. Not that haste was required to save a person, but because the more time that passed, the more the crime scene would be compromised. The body could have lain in the woods all night. If so, a lot of little critters would have taken the opportunity to have a snack.

Agent Hayes was in the passenger seat and Mayfield in the back before Shar had the key turned in the ignition. Good. They shared her need for speed. Pressing the gas pedal, Shar rocketed out of the parking lot and headed for Highland Springs' favorite necking spot.

She parked in a gravel lot and shoved open her door. A young couple in basketball shorts and tee shirts leaned against a rusty old Ford. Shar sighed to see the boy was Mason. Relief lit his face at the sight of her and he ran to her.

"It's awful, Sheriff. Louann is sick to her stomach. I need to take her home."

"Not until Deputy Mayfield takes your statement. I'm sorry." She clapped the boy on his shoulder. "I'm surprised you were allowed out after yesterday."

He ducked his head. "I snuck out."

"Alright. Go on now, while I attend to unpleasant business. Then you head straight home, hear me?"

"Yes, ma'am." He shuffled his feet back to his date and Mayfield.

"What happened yesterday?" Hayes held aside a low branch.

"Too much fun with a baseball bat and parked cars."

"And he's out of jail?" His eyes widened.

"No sense locking him up. His parents will make his life hard enough." Shar increased her pace toward the creek.

Yellow crime scene tape marked off a twenty-by-twenty square foot section. Lying in the middle of the tape was the sprawled body of a nude Rachel Holston. Her hands and feet were tied to stakes, stretching her as far as she would go. A senseless act of power after she was dead. Her cell phone lay next to her.

Shar closed her eyes for a moment to gain control of her rising anger. "The body does appear to be that of Rachel Holston, but we'll need a positive identification from the parents."

Hayes walked carefully around the perimeter. "A few prints, but my guess is they belong to your deputy and the youngsters. I doubt our killer would be that dumb."

Shar opened her mouth to reply, then snapped it closed at the sight of Lars Townsend, reporter for the one and only newspaper in town. The man was too talented for Highland Springs. She'd always wondered why he stayed.

"A comment?" He held his microphone in her direction.

"Nope." She turned her back. "Too soon for anything, Lars, and there had better not be a picture of this scene in this week's edition of the *Springs Gazette*, either." The poor victim didn't need to be remembered this way by her friends. The video was more than enough.

"I may be the press, but I'm not heartless." He leaned against a tree. "Who's that?"

"Federal Agent Everis Hayes."

"Called in the big guns?"

"He came to us."

Lars laughed. "That means this guy has killed before. I've got all I need for this week's paper, Sheriff. Thanks." He turned and motioned for his camera to follow him. Lars chose another spot of the creek to pose and acted as if he actually had something to say for the local station that aired at two a.m. when most folks were in bed.

"The angle he's filming will get part of the scene," Hayes said.

"The body?"

"I don't think so. Just the crime scene tape."

"That had better be all." Shar was more than fair with the citizens and expected the same treatment. "This is going to be a media circus."

⁕

Everis agreed. Once the recording went live or the paper hit the streets, every newspaper in the state and then some would descend on Highland Springs. The killer would thrive on the attention. "We have to keep this low-key. This man loves the attention."

She jerked to face him. "How do you know this?"

"The last murder went quiet after a few weeks. We had no leads, nothing. Then, he placed an ad in the paper saying his next show would be worthy of attention." He glanced at the body. "He was right."

"So, unless we give him a circus, make him a star, he'll up his game?"

Everis nodded. "I'm afraid so."

"Then I would think you'd make a big deal out of this in order to prevent another killing."

"I don't believe in caving to a psycho's demands."

She placed her fists on her hips. "I'll do whatever I have to in order to keep my people safe."

Perhaps working with the beautiful sheriff wasn't going to be as easy as he'd thought. Everis shrugged and returned to scanning the area for clues. He'd worked with prickly law enforcement before. Eventually, they discovered he had the authority to override them. Sometimes they became easier to work with, sometimes they didn't.

When they'd finished, Shar and Agent Hayes joined Mayfield who was typing his report on the sheriff's laptop. He glanced up as they approached. "I sent the kids home. They were pretty shaken up. Didn't have much to tell me other than they found her body, then called us."

"That's all they could have done." The sheriff resumed her place in the driver's seat. "Coffee?"

"Sounds good to me," Everis said, "unless you're talking about that stuff your receptionist makes. I'm sorry, but that stuff from the average coffee maker is either weak or strong. No happy medium."

"I keep meaning to buy a Keurig machine." Sheriff

Camenetti laughed. "Haven't gotten around to it. If I had one, I'd miss my morning trip to the coffee shop."

"You can still make your morning stop, but I'll make sure you have a coffee maker by morning." Everis shuddered.

"Then we'll make a pit stop and get something palatable."

So, the feds had arrived. The Silencer scowled. He thought he had at least a week. That Hayes was getting too close. He was like a pit bull, latching on two years ago and not letting go. The Silencer had hoped that lying low for a while would have shaken him off. Weren't there other killers to catch?

He drove home and locked all his doors and windows, making sure the shades were drawn. He needed a plan. He needed a victim. He needed to stay in the spotlight. The citizens of this Podunk town needed to be more frightened than they'd ever been. Evil things lived in the dark. His laugh rang across the living room. Highly intelligent beings such as himself.

He unlocked a door at the end of the hallway and went down a set of stairs into a portion of the basement that couldn't be found easily. His sanctuary.

He lit a candle in the center of the round wood table and stared at his reflection in the mirror. His eyes reflected the flickering of the candle's flames. He was a good-looking man. It was too easy to lure women into his web. One smile, some flowery phrases, and they were all his. He really did need more of a challenge.

He picked up a nearby knife, then ran the smooth side of the blade down his cheek. No, he enjoyed inflicting pain on others, not on himself. He wasn't that crazy. He smiled at his reflection, then sat at the table and booted up his computer. Facebook held a bevy of beauties at his disposal.

Choosing his next victim, he submitted a friend request.

CHAPTER THREE

Shar sat across from the victim's friend, Maggie Jensen, and couldn't help but feel the girl lied about the details of that morning. Maggie had shredded two napkins until a snowy pile sat on the table in front of her. Every time she had to answer a question, she refused to meet Shar's eyes.

"If you know something about Rachel's death, you are, under law, obliged to tell us." Shar leaned forward and folded her hands on the table. "I don't think you're being honest with us."

Maggie's eyes widened. "I am. I swear."

"Try again." Shar forced a smile. "You do know the Arkansas Bureau of Federal Investigations is now a part of solving this crime, right? I'll call in Agent Hayes if I must." He was listening from the other room with Maggie's parents, but the girl didn't need to know that.

Tears streamed down her face. "Okay. I guess it doesn't matter now anyway."

"What doesn't matter, Maggie?"

"Rachel was meeting a guy she met online. They would chat privately after meeting on Facebook." She heaved a sigh. "She was supposed to meet me at Dairy Queen, but texted that she was meeting him face-to-face for the first time."

"Do you know his name?"

She nodded and reached for her cell phone. "I even have a picture." She pulled up a black and white photo of a very handsome, very dead, Errol Flynn.

"I'll need to take your phone." Shar held out her hand. "This man has been dead for over fifty years. If you are contacted by someone you don't know, a new man wanting to be your friend, google him." She stood and marched out of the room to where Everis and Maggie's parents waited. "The man Rachel was meeting was Errol Flynn."

Everis stood. "At least the girl had good taste." He handed a business card to the parents. "Please stress the importance to Maggie of not meeting with anyone she doesn't know."

Shar headed outside, leaving Everis to follow. Across the street, Rachel's house, shades drawn, waited. She sighed and strode across the lawn to another unpleasant task, leaving Everis to catch up.

"He won't stop with Rachel," Everis said.

"I know."

"In fact, he probably already has his next victim picked out."

She stopped and faced him. "What's your point? If you have a better idea of what to do next in this investigation, then please feel free to share." The last thing she needed was the reminder that another of Highland Springs' young women would soon die at the hands of a madman.

Everis frowned. "I say we start monitoring all of Rachel's Facebook friends. See if any other women have Errol Flynn as a friend. See if any have other actors. We then focus on those women."

"The manpower this will require is staggering. I'll

have Mayfield start monitoring, but we'll need help."
Shar sent a message to her deputy and climbed the three
steps to the Holstons' porch. She rang the doorbell and
stepped back.

Mrs. Holston answered and held the door open.
"We've left her room just as she left it."

"Thank you. I know how difficult this is." Shar
stepped inside.

"Second door on the left." Mrs. Holston closed the
front door and retreated to the living room, leaving Shar
and Everis alone to do their work.

"I hate this part of the job." Shar climbed the stairs
and pulled on a pair of gloves.

The door to Rachel's room hung open. An unmade
queen-sized bed dominated the room. A closet stood
open, crammed with clothes. A dresser occupied one
wall, and under the window sat a desk. "I'll check out
the laptop."

Everis nodded. "I'll search through this…mess. She
definitely wasn't a neat freak."

"Most teenagers aren't." Shar booted up the
computer, but was immediately blocked by a password.
She groaned. "It's locked."

Everis leaned over her shoulder. A musky cologne
wafted from him, sending Shar's pulse racing and
threatening to distract her from the job at hand. There
should be a law against good-looking law enforcement.

"Try 1, 2, 3 ,4."

"Seriously?" Shar turned her head, her face almost
touching his, and returned her attention to the laptop.

"Most young people don't care about security."

Shar typed in the numbers. "Nope."

He glanced around the room. "Try Harry. It's the

name of her cat."

"It worked." Shar perched on the edge of the office chair and clicked on the Facebook icon. Seriously, who had over two thousand friends? "This will take forever. I'm going to focus on her profile page for now."

While Everis checked pockets of clothes hanging in the closet and riffled through drawers, Shar scrolled down Rachel's page. Not one picture of Errol Flynn. She moved to friend requests and scrolled down until she found his picture. She then went to instant messaging. Nothing. Their chats had to have been in a private chat room. She closed the laptop. A computer expert could get much further than she could.

"I found an address." Everis held up a slip of paper.

Shar took it from him. "This is a duplex on the outskirts of town. I recognize it from a domestic disturbance last month."

"Our mystery man's address, maybe."

"If only we could get that lucky." She pulled a baggie from her back pocket and held it open for Everis to drop the paper in. At least they knew their next step in the investigation.

* * *

Once they'd dropped the laptop off at the station, Everis drove them to the address he'd found in Rachel's jacket. He stared through the front windshield at a place that should have been condemned a long time ago. "People actually live here?"

Shar nodded. "I've been on the landlord to improve the living conditions, but it's cheap and some people can't afford more." She shoved her door open. "Highland Springs isn't exactly influential."

"My apologies. I wasn't judging." He exited the car.

"I seriously doubt Rachel would have been meeting with the Frasers, the couple I had a run-in with last month, so let's start with the other apartment." Shar knocked on the door. "Sheriff."

A young man opened the door and blinked sleepily up at them. "Yeah?"

"I'm Sheriff Camenetti and this is Agent Hayes. We'd like to ask you a few questions." Shar gave a thin-lipped smile.

"My dad's sleeping. He won't be happy if we wake him. Can we talk out here?"

Everis motioned to a lopsided picnic table. "This will do."

The boy led the way, then sat across from them. "What did he do this time?"

"Who?" Everis cocked his head.

"My dad."

"Why would you think he did anything?"

"He always does. Not usually here in town where people know us, but…" he shrugged.

"What's your name, son?"

"Thornton Hills." He grinned. "A fancy name for poor white trash, isn't it?"

"You're the only one who can make it mean something. Did you know Rachel Holston?"

His grin faded. "Yeah. We dated for awhile, until she said she'd found someone else. I heard she…died."

"Any idea who this new boyfriend was?"

Thornton shook his head. "Nah. She wouldn't return my calls anymore."

"What the hell is going on here?" A massive man with beefy arms and no neck stomped toward them. "Why is the sheriff questioning my boy without my presence?"

"I've got nothing to hide, dad." Thornton flinched.

Shar stood. "Mr. Hills, we're here in regard to the death of a young woman your son used to spend time with. We're hoping he might give us a clue to the identity of her killer."

Mr. Hills glowered. "Get off my property."

Everis stood and stepped between him and Shar. "Sir, this is public property. If you would prefer we take your son to the station for questioning, we can do that. Or, you can cooperate, as he is, and have a seat."

The man growled and plopped down next to Thornton. "My boy don't know nothing."

"That remains to be seen." Everis met Shar's stern glance, then nodded for her to resume her seat. As Everis sat, he unhooked the snap on the holster at his waist. "Thornton, when was the last time you spoke with Rachel?"

He thought for a moment. "Last week. The early part, I think."

"Did you frequent her Facebook page?"

"I did for a while, but then she blocked me."

Everis took a deep breath. "Why?"

The boy paled. "I threatened to make her sorry. I didn't kill her. I swear, I didn't."

Everis stared at the father and son long enough to make them both squirm. He knew neither of them killed the girl. Neither of them fit the physical build of the man on the tape. Still, it wasn't a good thing for any young man to threaten a young woman. He folded his arms and leaned across the table. "That was not wise, son. You keep up that type of behavior and some girl is going to file a complaint against you." He pulled back and slid a business card from his pocket. "Give us a call if you remember anything that might help us."

As he and Shar headed back to their vehicle, the reporter Lars hurried toward them. "Is that boy a suspect?"

"Are you following us?" Shar glared. "Not cool."

"How else am I supposed to find out anything?" Lars didn't look in the least bit ashamed. "Can I quote that you have a suspect?"

"No, because we don't." Everis took Shar by the elbow. "If you quote misinformation, the bureau will make sure you never write another news article."

He opened Shar's door. Instead of climbing in, she turned toward Lars. "Do not harass those people. They were nothing more than a lead."

If the man was smart, he'd pay heed to the hard glint in her eyes. Everis sure didn't want to be on the receiving end of that glare.

"If we find out anything, we'll let you know." He jogged to the driver's side and got in, before leaning across the still-empty passenger seat. "Are we on the same page, Mr. Townsend?"

The reporter's grin never faded. "Yep." Townsend stepped away from the vehicle and Shar took her seat. He waved as they drove away.

Everis glanced in his rearview mirror to see the reporter staring after them. "What are the chances he'll listen?"

"Not good. He'll head right for the Hills and start asking questions." She laughed. "Until Mr. Hills throws him off the property. I'd like to see that. Mr. Hill is a drunk and a bully, but he isn't a murderer." She cut Everis a sideways glance. "You don't suspect him, do you?"

"Wrong body shape. We're looking for someone my size." Someone filled with pure evil. A sociopath that walked among the innocent and preyed on his victims.

The Silencer watched the sheriff and the agent as they left with no clue as to his identity. They were like dogs chasing their tails. That's why he stayed in the Podunk town. He laughed and opened his laptop. It was a trip. He was getting away with murder. Entering a private chat room, he started a conversation with the lovely Amber and another with a delightful young woman by the name of Susy.

One of them would be his next star. Saved for eternity on film while their friends and family looked on. He could hardly wait. Only strong self-discipline kept him from asking one of them to meet him at that moment. No, it took time to win a woman's trust. As more died, it would become even harder. He relished the challenge.

Chapter Four

"Maybe I'm not cut out to be a sheriff." Shar sat on the front porch of her cabin and pushed the rocking chair into motion with her toe.

"Don't be stupid." Candy scowled. "You're perfect for the job. Just because you're stumped right now, doesn't mean you won't catch this guy. You need a haircut."

"Stop trying to get me under your scissors." Shar shuddered. There was no way she was letting the older sister she'd tormented through life have a go at her head.

"Fine. Let's talk about that FBI guy. He's hot." She grinned and took a sip from her glass of wine.

"We work together. That's all." But Candy was right about one thing. He was the hottest man to step foot in Highland Springs for...well, for as long as she could remember. His dark hair and eyes set a fire in her belly every time his gaze lingered on her for more than a split second.

"Speaking of." Candy leaped to her feet. "If you don't want him, can I have a go?"

Everis, teeth flashing in the moonlight, exited his rental car and approached the cabin. "Evening, ladies."

"Agent." Shar stopped rocking. "What can I help you with?"

His smile faded. "We've had another posting."

"I'm Candy, Shar's sister, and that's my cue to make myself scarce. I hope we can get to know each other another time." She thrust out her hand.

"My pleasure." He returned the shake and transferred his attention back to Shar. "I've my laptop in my car."

"Bring it into the kitchen. I'll make coffee." Shar stood and went in the house, leaving the front door open. Candy had already made herself comfortable in the living room and had put on a chick flick.

"This happened right on the heels of the other one," she said as Everis joined her in the kitchen.

He set the laptop on the table. "No, this one happened before Rachel."

"What?" She paused before putting a pod into the Keurig.

"A Susan Arnett, thirty-years-old, waitress in a bar." He turned the laptop around so she could see. "Her friends all thought it was a joke until they heard about Rachel's death."

"They weren't concerned when Arnett didn't show up for work?"

"Vacation."

She watched as a hooded man tortured and killed a pretty woman wearing shorts and a bikini top. While the victim screamed, the sound sharp and piercing, he fileted thin strips of skin from her thighs. "I wonder how many more there are."

"At least three that I know of. He didn't film the murders before, if it's the same guy I've been after, but torturing them before killing is the same."

"Where do we go from here? Can we set him up?

Make up a dummy social account?" She handed him the coffee and plopped in another pod for herself. "I can respond to posts, but we'd need someone else's profile picture. I'm too well known around here."

"We'll use an agent's picture. We can't put a civilian in that type of danger. Thanks for the coffee." He sat in the chair on the opposite side of the table.

Shar couldn't remember the last time a man was in her kitchen. Sure, Candy dated, but she never brought anyone home with her. Shar liked it that way. The fewer people who knew Shar's private side, where her sanctuary was, the better.

"Why would her friends think she was playing?" Shar sat across from Everis. "Those screams are real."

"I guess she was an aspiring actress and always goofing around for the camera. At least that's the story her roommate gave me. Do you have time to accompany me to their apartment in the morning?"

"I'm ready now." The more work they did, the sooner they'd catch this creep.

"She's working. As a single mother, she begged for us not to make her take off work." He gave a wry smile. "I can't resist a woman in distress. Besides, Susan has been dead a couple of weeks. A few more hours won't do anything." He stood. "Now, if you're up for a beer, that I can do."

Shar glanced toward the living room.

Candy gave her a wide-eyed glare that ordered Shar to go.

"Your sister can come."

"I don't turn down invitations from handsome men. Change your clothes, Shar." Candy headed up the stairs. "Five minutes."

Everis laughed. "I liked those tight jeans you wore the first time I saw you." He winked.

Shar's face heated. "They're in the laundry." She joined her sister upstairs and stared into her closet. The jeans were folded on the shelf. Shar smiled and grabbed a pair of denim jeans with holes in one thigh and another across the knee. Then, to top off the grunge look, she grabbed a tee shirt with the Beatles on the front.

"You are not wearing that." Candy crossed her arms over the tight shirt she wore. "Seriously, you look like a teenager."

"I don't see any reason to encourage a man's attention." She pulled the shirt over her head. "I'm focusing on my career."

"You're hiding." She whirled and stomped from the room.

Maybe she was. After the betrayal of the man she was going to marry ten years before, why waste time and emotion on another? Her life was full. She loved her job and her home. A woman didn't need anything more.

*
* *

Whoa. Everis didn't think anything could have been sexier than Shar in black, but her in tattered jeans and a faded tee shirt was the sexiest thing he'd ever seen. She wore her mane of ink-black hair hanging loose down her back. Her piercing blue eyes focused on his, taking his breath away. How did a man react to the challenge reflected in their depths?

He removed his tie and unbuttoned the top button. "I'll drive." He waved his arm. "After you, ladies."

He took them to a country/western bar he'd spotted

on the outskirts of town the other night. He planned on boot scootin' and boogying with Shar before the night was over. With a hand on the small of Shar's back, he guided her and her sister to a corner table. Candy was as sweet-looking as her name, but it was Shar's long-legs and curves that heated his blood.

"Three beers," he told the waitress.

"Cosmo," Shar said. "I don't like beer."

He clutched his heart. "Here I was hoping you'd lick it off my lips later."

Shar's eyes widened.

Her sister snorted.

The waitress left to place their orders.

"Shar doesn't know how to flirt." Candy tilted her head, clearly not like her sister.

"Why aren't either of the beautiful Camenetti sisters married?" Everis swept his gaze around the bar.

"This is where Arnett worked." Shar shook her head. "You won't interview the mother—"

"Who happens to be our waitress."

"—but you'll come here and scope out her job."

"I should have known it was too good to be true." Candy flounced against her chairback. "You're as big of a stick-in-the-mud as Shar. I'm going to find someone that's more fun." She sidled up to three men who were playing pool and soon she had a stick in her hand.

"She's a hairdresser. I don't think she'll ever understand exactly what law enforcement entails."

"A lot of people don't." He waited while the waitress brought their drinks, then directed her to take Candy's to her. "I thought maybe we could see who's here. See whether anyone pays any particular woman unwelcome attention."

She took a sip of her drink and set it precisely in the center of a napkin. "You don't think he meets them on social media?"

"I think he finds them out here, then hunts for them on social media." He studied the beautiful face next to him. "Why Highland Springs?"

Her features hardened. "Because I don't think the perp believes a woman is capable of catching him."

"Which means you resent me being here." He took a big swig of his beer. He didn't blame her. He'd stepped on her toes in an attempt to catch someone he'd been chasing for years.

She sighed. "It's not that. I'm not so shallow as to turn away help to prevent deaths for the sake of my ego. I do resent the fact that this killer chose my town. What other reason would he have?"

"Easy prey. In small towns, people aren't on guard like they are in larger cities. They're more trusting." He signaled for the waitress to bring another. "Let's take Candy as an example. She's completely carefree with three men she's probably never met."

"She's not shy."

"It's more than that. She's at ease." He pointed out the thrown-back head in laughter, the lack of normal flirtation—the batting of eyes or playing coy. "She's one of the guys as sexy as hell. They're all drooling over her, and she's acting like herself with no pretense. In the city, I'd bet twenty bucks she'd be more flirtatious. But here, she doesn't feel the need among good ole boys."

"Impressive."

"Let's dance. Two-step?" He stood and offered his

hand.

Her gaze clashed with his. "I do."

"Then, come on, Beatles fan. Let's move." He pulled her into his arms, his hand resting on the curve of her waist as they moved around the dance floor. She smelled of honeysuckle and felt better than any woman had a right to. When that song ended and a slow one played, he pulled her as close to him as was humanly possible and swayed to the music.

The Silencer watched the sheriff from his corner of the smoky bar. If his eyes hadn't witnessed how different she was from other women, she'd be his next victim. She'd be his masterpiece filming. But, she was nice, generous, compassionate. While she was firm in enforcing the law, she was fair, sometimes even lenient.

Her sister, on the other hand, was different. Loose and crass. Always chasing after the men in town. He curled his lip as her laughter rang out. If she were younger, he'd kill her. As it was, her youthful beauty was starting to fade. Approaching forty, it was sad how she clung to youth with colored hair and low-cut shirts.

His gaze drifted to the waitress. Ah, her friend had screamed the loudest of any of his victims. The sound thrilled him to the point he prolonged killing her. Then, when the fun faded, he silenced her. He ached to take another.

He'd chosen to woo them on social media so no one in town would ever see them together. Sometimes, a woman he wanted wasn't on social media. How was that possible in today's age? He shot back the last of his whiskey and grabbed his cowboy hat off the table. He smiled at the sheriff as he passed them. Her eyes were closed as she swayed in time to the fed.

It made The Silencer happy to see her relaxed. Relaxed meant she wasn't hunting him as hard as she should. And the sheriff should be hunting him, oh, yes, she should be hunting him with all that was in her.

Chapter Five

Funny how putting on a uniform made the night of dancing and drinking fade into the background. Shar pressed the doorbell to Susan Arnett's apartment and waited for her roommate to answer.

The waitress from the bar inched open the door. Shar cut Everis a quick glance, who grinned, then she asked, "Lucy Barnes?"

She sighed. "I've been expecting you. My son is in the living room watching cartoons. I hope you don't mind talking in the kitchen."

"Not at all." They followed her into an outdated kitchen with mismatched appliances.

"It isn't much, but it's home." Lucy motioned for them to have a seat. "I'm not sure what I can tell you."

Shar sat back and let Everis proceed with the questioning. It didn't take a genius to see that women responded better to a handsome man in a tie than they did to a woman in a sheriff's uniform. She glanced around the kitchen. Dirty dishes overflowed the sink and onto the counter. The trashcan lid didn't close. It was obvious Lucy was either busy, lazy, or never home.

"You told me on the phone that Miss Arnett went on vacation two weeks ago. Where did she go?" Everis's pencil poised over the pad in front of him.

"She was going to go to Eureka Springs and stay in

one of those tree houses."

Not very far away. Shar listened while continuing to run her gaze around the room, searching for anything that might be a clue.

"Why would you think something as horribly graphic as the video on her live feed was a prank?"

Lucy shredded a napkin in front of her. "She wanted to be an actress. One time, she dressed up as a...prostitute and roamed the seedy side of Little Rock. Just to see if anyone would pick her up. She always had someone taping her."

"Who?"

She shrugged. "Different people. I filmed her at the park once while she pretended to be an old woman feeding the birds. This was all supposed to be a part of her audition someday." Tears ran down her cheeks. "I did think the video of her...being murdered...was well acted."

It took a tremendous amount of self-control for Shar to keep her face impassive. Acting or not, she knew her sister well enough to know when something wasn't right. Lucy should have known her roommate better. Two weeks ago, Susan Arnett was brutally murdered, they had no bodies, and now another woman was dead. How long until The Silencer struck again?

Everis handed the woman a business card. "Call us if you think of anything that might help. Who she was with, who she was spending time with, phone calls, anything."

"Susan spent a lot of time on social media. Said she'd met someone. I thought she was meeting him in Eureka Springs." Lucy lowered her head. "She never made it there, did she?"

"We'll check the resort Ms. Arnett was planning to stay at and see whether she checked in." Shar stood, catching a glimpse of a boy around the age of four standing in the doorway of the kitchen. She smiled, relieved to see the worried look leave his face.

"Oh, sweetie." Lucy swiped her hand across her eyes. "This is grown-up talk."

"Aunt Susy got flowers."

Shar knelt in front of the boy. "She did? That's nice. Did you give them to her?"

"Nope. A man in a van did."

"Thank you." She turned to Lucy. "May we search her room?"

Lucy nodded. "The flowers must have come when she was watching Danny for me. Her room is the last door on the right. All I've done since she left was put her laundry on her bed."

A pile of unfolded laundry perched on top of an unmade bed. A vase of dead flowers sat on the nightstand. Sticking out of a plastic cardholder was a simple white card.

Shar pulled a rubber glove from her pocket, snapped it on, and took the card. "See you tonight."

Everis peered over her shoulder, giving her a whiff of cologne that sent her pulse racing. "I don't think she made it to Eureka Springs."

All it would take was to move her head an inch and he'd be within kissing distance. She took a deep shuddering breath, praying he didn't notice how he affected her. Being a woman sheriff was hard enough without her fawning over an agent. Shar picked up a brochure with a picture of cabins nestled among the trees. "I agree, but we'll contact this place anyway."

She called Mark on the radio asking him to gather some people together and scour the woods near where they'd found Rachel. "Take some search dogs. We'll join the hunt when we're finished here."

Everis stepped a few feet away and dialed the number on the brochure. "Susan Arnett's room, please." His gaze locked with Shar's. He listened, then shook his head. "Thank you." A shadow crossed his face. "She never checked in."

"With no idea of when she left, who she was meeting, or what route she planned to take, we're fishing in the dark without a flashlight." Shar slipped both the card and the brochure into a paper sack. "Maybe we can get someone to find something, anything, on her laptop."

"We will find this guy, Shar."

"Not before he kills someone else."

"Do you want to meet somewhere?" The Silencer talked to his latest in a private chat.

"Too scary. LOL."

"Scary?"

"Some creep is killing women online."

He smiled. He was becoming famous. "It's not me. LOL."

"How would I know?" A smiley face appeared. "We just started talking two days ago."

He'd moved too fast. Time to backpedal. "It's wise to be cautious. It's hard to be patient while waiting for a beautiful woman, but I can do it."

"A sweet talker."

"Can I have our real name?"

"You first."

The Silencer laughed. This pretty little thing wasn't as dumb as she looked. "Bill Johnson."

"Hello, Bill. I'm Amber. Let's take this slow, okay?"

The Silencer slapped his laptop closed. If she wasn't going to be an easy mark, he needed to find someone else. Meeting someone other than online was risky. Faces could be recognized.

He leaned back in his office chair and studied all the idiots slaving away around him. People too blind to see that he was so far above their station he'd be remembered someday. Remembered for a very long time.

Without a word to anyone, he grabbed his car keys and headed out. His hunger needed to be fed.

Everis drove to the hiking path that circled the lake and parked in the same lot they'd parked in when finding Rachel's body. It was plausible the killer would dump his victims in close proximity with each other but, while not new at killing, he was evolving. This case was going to test every investigative skill Everis and the lovely sheriff had.

"What's wrong?" Shar turned to face him.

"I've been chasing this guy for so long I should know what his next move will be. Except I don't. He stays one foot ahead of me." He shoved open his door. "Let's see if we can't make up a few inches of that foot."

"At least you've done this before," she said catching up with him. "I've not had to deal with anything more difficult than a domestic dispute. I keep up on the latest and greatest ways to catch a killer, but

I've never had to put them to the test. I feel very inadequate." She groaned. "I cannot believe I admitted that out loud."

"You're feeling inadequate because of never having to deal with anything of this magnitude." He crooked his mouth.

"Yes." She met his gaze. "Sheriff is an elected position. I love my job, and I love this town. If we don't catch this guy…

"I understand." He put a hand on her shoulder and gave a gentle squeeze. "We'll catch him."

"So you keep saying."

"If I stop saying those words, it means I've given up." He headed for the hiking trail they'd taken before. He didn't intend to give up. Not ever. The families of the victims deserved justice, at the very least,.

"Hey, boss." Deputy Mayfield strolled toward them. "Nothing within fifty feet of where we found Holston's body."

"Keep looking. Widen the search area." Shar marched down the path and stood at the water's edge.

Everis kept an eye on her pine-tree straight back and squared shoulders. He recognized a fighter's stance. Leaving her to her thoughts, he headed away from the path and deeper into the woods. The forests of the Ozarks had plenty of hiding places to stash a body. They'd find Susan Arnett.

"What are you looking for today?" The newspaper reporter, Townsend—Everis thought his name was— came down the path with camera in hand.

"The body of Susan Arnett."

"Another one?"

"She was killed before Rachel Holston. I can't tell

you more than that." Everis kept walking. The sheriff might not be happy he'd said as much as he had, but the public needed to know there was a serial killer at large. Knowledge was safety.

"Can I quote you that there are two victims? When did the first victim die?"

"We won't know that until we locate her body and have the ME take a look." Everis studied a scuff mark on the ground. Using the toe of his shoe, he moved leaves aside, revealing the telltale tracks of something being. He put two fingers between his lips and gave a shrill whistle.

"You need to leave now, Mr. Townsend. We can't have you contaminating what might be a crime scene. I'm sure your DNA is all over the place now."

"I'll stay a safe distance back." Townsend stepped a few feet away.

"Farther." Shar stepped past him and joined Everis. "Find something?"

"I think so." Everis followed the drag marks, careful not to step on them until he came to a slight overhang in the mountainside. From the rotting odor emanating from underneath, he guessed they'd found Arnett. "Get the crime scene techs in here."

Shar made a call on her radio, then ordered Mark to secure the area. "Townsend, move back. I'm not going to tell you again."

The man saluted and took another two steps back. Everis shook his head. It was only a matter of time before the reporter pissed Shar off and she arrested him to make a point.

Everis pulled on a pair of gloves and picked up a stick. Using the end of it, he parted the limbs piled in an attempt to mask a hiding place. A decaying hand with bright red fingernails fell out. "We definitely have a body."

Shar bent over and peered into the space under the overhang. A strand of hair had fallen out of Shar's ponytail and blew across Everis's face. He breathed deep of her lemon-scented shampoo. He would have liked to have met her under different circumstances. No other woman stirred his blood the way she did.

Yanking his attention back to the job at hand, he planted his hands on his thighs and pushed to his feet. There had to be a clue as to who had put the woman here. He glanced upward through the trees. Why did God allow such evil in the world?

"What are you looking for?" Shar looked up.

"Life's answers."

She chuckled. "Good luck with that." She walked away, her gaze sweeping the area. "Everis."

He hurried to her side and peered at the very distinct size ten-and-a-half shoe print. "This could possibly be our strongest clue as to the identity of The Silencer."

She blew air through her nose. "I'm going to silence him before this over."

Everis nodded. Shar and him both.

Chapter Six

With coffee in one hand and feet propped on the conference table, Shar stared at the case board. What were they missing? No one does anything without leaving a trace, yet The Silencer was like a ghost, vanishing into the mist after every kill.

"Hey, boss." Mayfield stood in the doorway. "Got some teens skipping school and smoking pot out by the lake. Want me to handle it?"

"No, I'll do it. I need a break. See if you can make sense out of this board." Maybe something would click into place for one of them. Shar nabbed her jacket and met Everis on the way. "Want to meet some local youth?"

"Sure." He grinned, his dark eyes sparkling—sucking her in, promising heaven.

Stop it, Shar. Man, she must be lonelier than she thought. "I'll drive."

"My pleasure." He followed her outside and climbed into the passenger seat of her jeep. "What's the call?"

"Kids smoking pot at the lake. Happens on a regular basis." She turned the key in the ignition and drove the five miles to the waterfront.

They could smell the weed before coming upon the group of teens sitting on the shore. The kids were so engrossed in giggling and passing the joint, they didn't notice Shar and Everis until Shar cleared her throat.

Curses and shrieks filled the air. Someone tossed the last of the joint into the water. They jumped to their feet and prepared to run.

"Don't even think about it or I'll have the agent shoot you." Shar sighed heavily. "Someone get that trash out of the water before it dissolves and I add littering to the list of wrongs you've done here today."

One boy bent over to retrieve the joint from the water only to have it fall apart in his fingers. He stared up at Shar with wide eyes.

Everis chuckled and leaned close to Shar. "Kind of like…oh, crap, now what? I like small town life."

Shar fought back a smile. She'd laugh at the silliness later. "How in the heck am I supposed to get you all to the station?" There were ten miscreants in all. "You won't fit in my jeep—"

A girl raised her hand. "We could follow you," she said in a small voice.

"Like that would really happen. Line up and give me your names. I'll call your parents and have them bring you down." Letting their parents know what their kids had been up to when they were supposed to be at school would be a huge punishment. "You'll all be doing community service. If you don't show up to find out where I've assigned you, then I'll arrive at your house with pretty, silver handcuffs. Got it? Everyone, look at me and nod if you understand."

Ten heads nodded.

"I won't let you drive yourselves home, so Agent Hayes will babysit you while I step over there and call a school bus to come get you."

"How will we get our cars?" Someone asked.

"That's not my concern. I'm sure when you get off the bus at home, your parents will be more than happy to help. Smoking marijuana is against the law. Consider this a warning." Shar stepped away and turned her back to the group. Laughter bubbled up inside her. She'd been one of them once, and a law enforcement officer had given her the same opportunity to straighten up. She'd taken it, and now look at her. She placed a call to the school requesting a bus, then went back to help Everis babysit.

By the time the bus arrived, he knew everyone's name, had written them down, and had even taken the time to counsel a young man with a misdemeanor record as long as his arm. Highland Springs could use a man like Hayes on a regular basis.

Shar and Everis watched the kids file up the stairs and into their seats. The bus driver barked orders for them to each sit alone, then closed the doors. Once the bus was out of sight, Shar let the laughter she'd been holding in escape.

"I love this town."

"Most sheriffs would have arrested them on the spot."

"I will if they get caught again. I'm not stupid. They're going to smoke and nothing I say will change that. Maybe now, they'll be a little smarter and responsible about it." She started down the path to her jeep.

Everis fell easily into step with her. "I admire your empathy. I really do. Maybe if more law enforcement officers gave kids another chance, by involving their families, more would stay out of trouble."

Shar chuckled. "They'll regret getting caught. Their parents will make sure of that, and the community service I have planned is very unpleasant. We have a garbage dump, a food kitchen, trash on the side of the road, sidewalks on Main Street that need sweeping, fire trucks that could use a good washing—those might be for repeat offenders, who will get the nastier jobs of Community service every weekend for three months. That ought to take care of the problem." She pressed the fob on her keyring, unlocking the doors. "Break is over. Back to catching a killer."

He shrugged. "I much preferred dealing with the high kids."

So did she.

Back at the office, Amber sat behind her desk, frowning at her computer screen. "Take a hint, dude."

"Something wrong?" Shar paused on her way to the conference room.

"Some guy I met online."

Shar speared Everis with a look, then turned back to Amber. "What does he want?"

"To meet me."

Shar swallowed past the mountain in her throat. "Come with us to the conference room. Turn off your computer."

Everis tried to give Amber a reassuring smile, but the cold rock in his stomach most likely made it look like a grimace.

Her eyes widened as she followed Shar's orders, then clip-clopped after her on clear plexiglass heels that reminded him of what a stripper might wear. Some of the coldness left him as he smiled and followed the women into the conference room.

He closed the door behind him. Mayfield, who stood at the case board with hands clasped behind him, turned and eyed Amber, then Shar. "What's going on?"

"That's what we're about to find out. Amber, you aren't in trouble. Please, have a seat." Shar glanced at Everis, giving him permission to lead the questioning.

He sat down across from the nervous receptionist and folded his hands on the table top. "Let's start from the beginning."

"Of what?" She bit one bright red lip and cut a glance to Shar.

This wouldn't be easy. Where did Shar find her? "The meeting of your mystery man."

"Oh." She drew the word out. "Social media. He requested to be friends and since he's hot, I said yes."

"Do you have a picture of this man?"

She pulled up a picture on her cellphone and turned it toward Everis. "Dreamy, right?"

"Very, considering that's the actor known as Doctor Dreamy on a television show."

"Oh." Her face fell. "He's been lying to me?"

"It appears so. Amber, you work here. Surely, you're aware of the man who is murdering women he meets online."

"Of course." She frowned. "That's why I won't meet him yet."

"You won't meet him at all. What did he say his name was?"

"Bill Johnson."

Everis doubted that was the man's real name. "Did you give him your real name?"

"Yes." Tears welled in her eyes. "Is he going to

come after me?"

Everis met Shar's gaze. He had a problem with crying females. They left him feeling helpless and unable to say anything coherent.

"Amber, I need you to delete your social media account and take a vacation. While on that vacation, I need you to call me three times a day. I'm also going to put a tracker on your phone." Shar rolled her head on her shoulders to get the kinks out. "Do you understand?"

"My car is in the shop."

"I'll have Detective Mayfield drive you wherever you want to go, then rent you a car."

Everis's admiration of the beautiful sheriff increased every time he had the opportunity to witness her with a civilian. She might be tough as nails when she needed to be, but beating under that sheriff uniform was a soft heart.

"Hand me your phone," Shar said. She then gave it to Mark. "Make sure the social media account is deleted and a tracker put on. Then, take Amber home to pack."

"How long do I have to go away?" Amber sniffed.

"Until we catch this guy."

She nodded and followed Mark.

Shar sat back in her chair. "I know we could have used Amber as bait, but I can't do that. No one will be used in that capacity but me."

"I agree." Everis moved to the sideboard and poured two cups of coffee, added cream and sugar, then handed one to Shar. "Where did you find Amber?"

"I found her on the streets." Shar smiled. "She's a bit flighty, but answers phones well. She's friendly, and knows how to work on the computer. Unfortunately, I haven't been able to get her to sway too far from her former style of clothing." She laughed.

"Let's set up that profile for you." Everis pulled a laptop close, hating that Shar was willing to step into danger. The man they were after was good. Very good. If he found out her deception, it could send him into a rage. "Here's the photo you'll use for your profile pic." He showed her a picture of a female agent. Thirty, brunette, blue eyes. The perfect target. Except the target wasn't going to be the nameless agent, it would be Shar. "Natalie Larson will be here tomorrow. I was going to get her a temporary job somewhere else, but she can take over Amber's job as receptionist for now." He sent Nat a text. "The perp knows the women of this town. He gets their name, looks them up, and sends a friend request. It's easy."

"She's the face, I'm the one he'll be corresponding with. This should work." Shar's fingers flew over the keyboard. "It's easy enough to spread around that Amber left for a family emergency."

He doubted that. "I'm sure everyone in this town knows everyone."

"Except who The Silencer is."

Amber's profile was gone. The Silencer cursed. He called the station. The sheriff answered.

He hung up. She would know his voice.

He'd have to find out about Amber some other way. He drummed his fingers against his lips. Who would know?

He should have gone with his gut instinct and outright asked her for a date using his real identity. The silly girl would have said yes. But, she might have told someone she was going on a date with him. That had stilled his hand. Now, she wasn't online or behind the phone.

She'd left town. Why? There was no way she could know she was a target. He slammed his hand against his desk, ignoring the startled glances of his fellow workers. Now, he'd have to set his sights on someone else. It sometimes took weeks to groom a woman. To get her to trust him enough to want to meet him.

His hunger was growing stronger. He hadn't taken a stranger in a very long time, but he might have to resort to one temporarily.

But who could he take? Should he wander the streets after dark...ah, yes. He knew what he'd do. He finished the day's work and shut off his computer. He had preparations.

Whistling, he loosened his tie on the way to his car and headed home. He had the perfect tools in his workshop and could whip up what he needed in ten minutes. Wood, nails, and a lonely road would give him what he sought.

Chapter Seven

The Silencer was taking a chance that the next car to come down that road was a woman, but it was after five o'clock. Women would be returning home from work, and he'd scouted the area well enough to suspect that a single woman lived at the next house. He'd seen no signs of a man or a child when he snooped around the property. He set out the homemade nail strip and waited in the shadows. He smoked two cigarettes, grinding the butts into the damp ground and covering them with leaves. Let the squirrels get cancer.

The anticipation of catching prey was almost as invigorating as luring a woman through cyberspace into meeting him. Headlights appeared over the hill. He rubbed his hands together, almost giggling from the joy. Oh, he might have just found a new game to play.

The dark red sedan drove over the nails. An audible pop reached The Silencer's ears. He clapped as the car careened into the ditch. Showtime.

He jogged to where he'd hidden his car, then drove over the hill, avoiding the nails, and pulled onto the shoulder. He waited to see whether the woman would leave the safety of her vehicle. She did.

He opened his door and, without getting all the way out, said, "Car trouble?"

"I ran over something. I have two flat tires, but only

one spare."

Pretending to be concerned, he marched to where he'd laid the strip, then tossed it into the bushes to retrieve later. "No idea what you hit. A sharp rock, maybe?" He knelt and peered under her car. "I don't see anything. Can I give you a lift?"

He caught a glimpse of his victim. While not as pretty as the others, she was pleasant, a bit plump. The thrill of anticipation over catching her ruled out her lack of beauty. Yes, he'd have a good time with this one.

"I, uh…" She glanced up the road. "I don't live far. It's no trouble to walk."

"Okay." He shrugged and glanced at the heels on her feet. "Have a good day." He started for his car.

"Wait. All right. Let me get my purse."

Within minutes, she sat quietly in his passenger seat. Her shyness was endearing. Too bad she'd be screaming soon. In fact, he planned on killing her in her home and leaving her body there to be discovered. Wouldn't that throw the lovely sheriff a curve? Him going off his MO?

"I'm Bill Johnson," he said when they stopped in front of her small house. "Are you on social media?"

"Yes." She ducked her head. "It's the most socializing I do."

"A pretty thing like you? Hey, do you mind if I use your restroom? I got pretty dirty looking under your car."

She cut him a quick glance. "I suppose that would be okay." She exited the car and climbed the steps to her front door.

The Silencer pulled on a pair of leather gloves.

The moment the key turned in the latch, The

Silencer shoved her inside, hitting her over the head with the nearest object at hand. A crystal vase from the foyer table.

She crumbled like a wadded piece of garbage. The Silencer dragged her to the dining room and hefted her onto the kitchen table. Using cords he found around the house, he secured her, then rummaged through her kitchen drawers for a sharp knife. Finding one, he set it on the table next to her. He dug her cellphone from her purse, logged into her social media, then propped the phone against a salt and pepper shaker. This was going to be glorious.

He pulled his mask from his pants pocket and waited for her to wake up.

* * *

"Shar." Everis stepped into her office. "I'd like to introduce you to your new receptionist, albeit temporarily. Natalie Larson."

Shar stood and shook the pretty brunette's hand. She was dressed professionally in a dark pencil skirt and pretty, light blue blouse. So different from dear Amber. "Welcome aboard. We can sure use your help in catching this creep."

"Looking forward to it." She smiled, then left, leaving them alone.

"She doesn't look like an agent." Shar resumed her seat behind her desk.

"That works to our advantage. We've used her undercover in a ton of situations where a fresh young face is needed."

"Let's keep that pretty face from getting cut up." She nodded as a stern-faced couple was escorted past her door. "Time to meet the parents. Coming?"

He shook his head. "No, I'm headed back to the two crime scenes. We have to have missed something."

"Good luck." She flashed a smile, grabbed a notebook, and headed for the conference room. These were her people. This was something she could do.

"Good afternoon, Mr. and Mrs. Thompson. Lyle." She sat across from them and opened the notebook. "I trust Lyle has told you why you came here?"

"Ditching school and smoking pot." Mr. Thompson bopped his son in the back of the head. "Deserves a lot more than whatever you're going to do to him."

"First off, no beating your kid while I'm watching." She grinned, knowing Lyle was the least mistreated kid in town. Born with a silver spoon in his mouth, he thought he was above having to do work. "Now, legally, I have every right to arrest your son. But I'm willing to help him make better choices. Lyle, I'll be checking with each of your teacherson your attendance every day. You have an eight o'clock curfew for ninety days." She held up a hand as he opened his mouth. "Non-negotiable. For twelve weekends, you will work at the town garbage dump weeding out recyclables starting this weekend. Any questions?"

The sullen boy shook his head. His mother's face paled, but his father grinned like someone who'd just caught the biggest fish.

"That ought to teach the scamp." He leaned his elbows on the table. "I trust the others are receiving similar punishments?"

"Not that I'm at liberty to say, but they are all receiving the same terms with different community service projects." Shar stood. "Good day."

Her day continued on in the same fashion, most

parents being more than happy to comply with their child's punishment. Only one couple complained because of having to cancel family plans.

Her cell phone rang. Everis. "Hey."

"I'm where we found Arnett. Do you have time to meet me here?"

"Be there in fifteen." Click.

"Heading out, Natalie. I've got my cell. Numbers on your desk pad." Shar rushed out the front door.

"Sure thing, Sheriff." She reached for the ringing phone. "Hold up." She held up a finger and finished with the call. "Stay there, sir. The sheriff is on her way." She hung up the phone and turned back to Shar. "UPS man caught sight of a bloody woman tied to her kitchen table. Thought it might be more important than what the agent has."

"They're both important. Where's Mayfield?"

"On the drive back from dropping off Amber." Natalie grinned. "The girl wanted to go to Nashville. I've texted you and Agent Hayes the address of the body."

"Thanks." Shar dashed outside to her jeep, calling Everis on her way. "Meet me at the address just texted to you. We'll head back to the scene of Arnett's death later."

"Gotcha."

Shar turned on her police lights and sped toward the address given. She made note of a car sitting half in the ditch before pulling into a gravel driveway next to a UPS truck. A visibly shaken man smoked a cigarette, his hand trembling so bad it took several attempts for him to get the correct end in his mouth. Taking note of the other butt on the ground, she declined telling him not to contaminate the scene. The damage outdoors had been done.

While waiting for Everis, Shar stepped up to the large window and cupped her hands around her eyes. A woman lay sprawled on the table, her arms and legs tied with what looked like extension cords. A cell phone sat propped against a salt and pepper shaker, the lens trained on the wide-eyed stare of the dead woman. With her hand on her weapon, Shar searched the perimeter of the house.

Finished, she approached the driver. "Do you usually look in the windows of the houses where you drop packages?"

"I do when it's Nell's." He tried lighting another cigarette.

Shar took the lighter and lit it for him. "Why?"

"She's addicted to Amazon. I probably deliver a package a day except for Sundays. Plus, I knew she was off-work today, but when I saw her car in the ditch, I thought it strange she didn't open the door when I knocked, so I looked in the window to see if she was alright. She isn't." He turned and vomited near the driver's front wheel.

Everis pulled to a stop behind Shar's jeep and climbed out. "Whose car in the ditch?"

"The victim's." Shar motioned her head for him to follow her to house. "The homeowner is inside, clearly dead, tied to a table. Same MO as the others with regard to skin being removed. Other than that, nothing's the same except the phone being used to record."

He frowned. "It can't be a copycat. No one knows enough details."

"Doors are locked. I walked the perimeter, but…"

"Nell keeps a spare key in that birdhouse." The UPS man pointed at a bird feeder resembling an outhouse that hung from the porch eave.

Shar snapped on a pair of gloves and retrieved the key. "Don't leave, sir. We'll need to take your statement."

She unlocked the front door and stepped inside, hand on her weapon. "Sheriff. Anyone home?" Silence greeted them.

Relaxing her grip, she stepped into the dining room. A quick study of the cellphone showed it was still recording and was tuned into social media. A charger kept the camera juiced up. Keeping her face expressionless, she peered into the lens, then shut off the camera. "He's taunting us."

"This poor woman's family and friends were subjected to this sight for hours." Everis peered at the body. "Cute, but not as pretty as his usual victims."

"Why let him into her house?" Shar roamed the room, noting the bloody knife in the sink. "He used her things. We need to take a look at the car."

"I'm right behind you."

After calling a cab for the UPS driver and promising to take his statement later, they drove to the abandoned vehicle. It didn't take Everis long to determine the reason it ran off the road.

"Both tires are flat."

Shar rolled her shoulders, trying desperately to ease the tension. "He put something in the road, hid in the trees, and somehow convinced her to let him give her a ride." She peered through the car window. "No keys, no purse, cleaner than I ever keep my jeep." She stepped back and watched as Everis paced the tree line, his gaze darting from one spot on the ground to another.

"Here. Something was tossed here. See the crushed grass?" He pointed to a four-foot, narrow path. "Here's the same ten-and-a-half shoe prints." He bent and picked up a stick, carefully moving leaves. "Bingo."

"What?" Shar stepped next to him.

"I found a cigarette butt near where Arnett was found. Same brand as these."

Shar grinned. "Our first clue, and it might be a doozy."

"Let's go finish casing the scene. You really need to hire more officers."

"I don't usually have this type of crime." She'd been on the state for years to give her even two more. It took a lot out of her to be sheriff, crime-scene investigator, bearer of bad news, and anything and everything in between. Still, she couldn't imagine doing anything else. "Why don't you talk to the bigwigs for me." She clapped him on the shoulder. "Enough dreaming, let's find justice for these women."

Chapter Eight

Shar stood behind the podium in front of the red-brick sheriff's office. She hated giving press releases, but it was time she addressed the evil terrorizing her town.

She tapped the microphone and waited for the piranhas, aka news reporters, to settle down. "As you know, we've had three women killed in Highland Springs within the last month. We are closing in on a suspect..." Liar. "but for the safety of the investigation, I cannot go into further detail."

Lars raised his hand. "Will you be enforcing a curfew?"

"Not at this time. We encourage women not to go anywhere alone or arrange to meet with anyone they don't know."

A reporter from Little Rock asked, "I've heard you're calling the killer The Silencer. Is this true?"

Shar nodded. "That seems to be what he wants to be called." She stared into the cameras. "I'd rather call him a coward." Her gaze flicked to Everis. He had specifically told her not to antagonize the killer. She couldn't help it. The suspect needed to be drawn into the open.

Everis shook his head, his expression let Shar know

without words that he'd have plenty to say when they were inside.

"Your receptionist has disappeared," Lars said. "Is she a victim?"

"She's left town for a family emergency and will return soon. No more questions. Thank you." Shar spun around and entered the building while reporters called out to her. The closing of the door effectively shut off their comments, only to be reawakened when Everis entered.

"I thought we agreed you wouldn't call him out." His eyes flashed. "It does no one any good for you to go off half-cocked on some kind of Lone Ranger act."

"Half-cocked? Please." She marched to her office. "I thought you wanted to catch this guy."

"I do." He stormed after her, slamming her office door after him. "That's why Natalie is here. That's why you're monitoring the social media."

She sat in her chair and glared. "An angry killer is a stupid killer. One who makes mistakes like leaving cigarette butts at the scene of the crime."

"We suspect it was the killer." He plopped into the chair across from her. "We won't know for sure until we have DNA."

"It's the best lead we have." Shar refused to be swayed. She would face this killer sooner than later and save the women of Highland Springs.

Natalie knocked on the door and entered when Shar waved her in. "I've found the woman from yesterday's feed. It's gone viral. He filmed her from the moment he tied her up until you turned off the camera. Ten hours of footage." She set a laptop on Shar's desk.

"Some people are sick." Shar watched as The

Silencer made Nellie Wilson scream. His smile widened under the ski mask he wore. She wanted this man caught and sentenced to death.

"You also received this in today's mail." Natalie handed her an evidence bag. "I open the mail gloved." She flashed a grin. "This was addressed to you."

Shar reached for the bag. "Have that taping taken down immediately. Anything from forensics on an IP address on any of these tapings?"

"Coffee shops, fast food places, anywhere that offers free Wi-Fi."

"Thanks, Natalie." Shar pulled a single sheet printed on regular copy paper from the envelope and read out loud to Everis.

"My dearest Sheriff,

Are you having fun yet? I am having so much fun it should be illegal. Oh, wait, it is! LOL. We have a connection, you and I. Can you guess what it is? No? I'll be leaving you clues at each scene of a lovely woman's death. Have you found the first ones? The Silencer."

"It's nothing but a game to him." Everis ran his hands through his hair. The strands fell back into place.

How did he do that? Look so perfect all the time? "The cigarettes must be the clue he's talking about. We scoured the crime scenes and didn't find anything else."

"How would they tie into you?"

"I have no idea. I've never smoked."

"What about your parents?"

She picked up a pen and started doodling on her desk pad. Pain accompanied talking about her parents, what she knew of them. "Mom drank a lot and my father left when I was two. Mom said he'd sleep with any woman that would have him."

"Do you have photos?"

"Somewhere at home." She stood. "Come on. It's a long shot, but I don't have any other ideas."

"Let's grab lunch first, my treat."

"You're on. I want a juicy burger with a large diet coke and a mountain of French fries."

He laughed. "Lead the way."

How could she eat so much and look so darn good? Everis watched in appreciation as she headed down the hall.

"Caughtcha looking." Natalie smiled up from her desk. "Careful. You're leaving when this guy is caught."

"I have no idea what you're talking about." He gave her a salute and jogged to catch up with Shar.

Yes, he knew this was only a temporary assignment, but there was nothing to say he couldn't make the two-hour drive once in a while. It wouldn't exactly be a long-distance relationship.

Did he want a relationship? None had ever lasted. The women always wanted more than he could give. They couldn't handle the demands of his job, and he hadn't cared enough to change. Dare he hope Shar might be the woman to change his outlook?

They drove to a dive of a burger shop where the only seating was outside. "What do y'all do in the winter?"

Shar grinned. "Portable heaters. Sometimes the owner lowers clear plastic tarps if it's cold and windy. It's worth it."

They chose a table with mismatched lawn chairs off

to the side and studied a laminated menu before a chirpy waitress in black pants and a bright yellow blouse approached them. "What can I get you?"

"Two bacon cheeseburgers, two large fries," Shar drummed her fingers on the tabletop, "I want a diet, but…"

"I'll take a regular coke," Everis said. "I'm assuming half of that order is for me."

"I wanted you to try the best thing on the menu." Shar sat back, clearly not caring what he thought about her ordering for him.

It didn't matter. He liked a strong woman. Folding his arms on the table, he said, "Let's brainstorm any possible ways you can be connected to The Silencer."

"Fine. Ruin lunch." She smiled. "My mother smoked, but I seriously doubt she's the killer. I'm the youngest of two, as far as I know. My father probably smoked. He drank as well from what Mom said, but he would have to be in his mid-to-late fifties."

"Doesn't mean he isn't capable of killing anyone." He hated the shock of pain that flickered across her eyes. No one wanted to entertain the notion that a family member might be a serial killer. "We're just speculating here, Shar."

"I know. But, I can't think of any other way to be connected other than by family."

"Maybe we'll find something in pictures. It's a long shot, but if we see Marlboro Reds, then we might have something."

Lars popped around the building. "The Silencer smokes? So does half the population of Highland Springs. You'll have to do better than that, Sheriff."

Shar narrowed her eyes. "If you print any of that,

I'll arrest you for—"

"I know. Obstruction of justice. You sure make it hard for a guy to get a story." He pulled up a chair and sat down as the waitress placed their order in front of them. Grabbing a fry from Shar's plate, he continued, "I mean, the public deserves to know what's going on. Maybe one of them have seen this guy, but don't realize it. The more details, the more chances they'll remember."

Everis, while shocked at the man's audacity to take food from a hungry woman's plate, sat back to enjoy the show. Shar was definitely right about one thing. The burger was the best he'd eaten in a very long time.

"Look, Lars." Shar slapped his hand as he reached for another fry. "Get your own food and stop following me around and eavesdropping. Seriously. You're a thorn in my side."

The man laughed. "Come on. I voted for you. Throw me a bone."

"Here's your bone." There was hint of evilness to her smile. "The killer is a man."

"Come on." Lars flounced back against the chair. "Everyone who watches the video knows that."

"Don't watch the video." Everis speared the reporter with his gaze. "The more people who watch, the more it fuels him. The man thrives on the attention. You can write that in your article."

Lars studied him for a minute. "You're a smart one, Agent Hayes. I'll quote you on that statement. Sheriff, something I can use?"

She sighed. "I'm asking that women stay offline. I know they won't, so please stress that they entertain caution."

"Not very noteworthy, but it's something." He stood. "Thanks. I'll be around."

"Unfortunately," Shar muttered.

The reporter laughed again, wrote something on a notepad he pulled from his back pocket and left.

"Persistent, devil, isn't he?" Everis wiped his mouth with his napkin, then tossed it on his plate. "Ready?"

Shar's sister Candy arrived home the same time they did. "Hey, Agent. Looking good."

"You're always good for my ego." Everis laughed and swung his arm around her. "You off work?"

"Lunch break." Her gaze switched to Shar's. "What's up?"

"Did Dad smoke?"

"Sure, he did. Like a chimney. Why?" She slipped from under Everis's arm and climbed the steps.

"Do you know what kind?" Shar asked.

Candy glanced over her shoulder. "What's this about? I was five-years-old when he left. Of course, I don't remember what brand."

Shar ushered her into the house, leaving Everis to follow. "You cannot tell anyone, Candy. I mean it."

"I've kept the secrets until now, haven't I?"

"The killer smokes Marlboro Reds."

She frowned, tossing her keys on a foyer table and heading for the kitchen. "You think our old man is the killer?"

"We're just going through our options," Everis said. "Would you mind getting those pictures, Shar?"

"I'll be right back."

Everis watched as Candy prepared a sandwich, declining when she offered him one. "You were older when your father left. Do you remember any mention of cousins, uncles…?"

"No. Mom never said anything either." She sat across from him. "Not that that means anything. Mom stayed in a fog most of the time. Shar and I pretty much fended for ourselves."

"Sometimes the neighbors fed us," Shar said, setting a shoebox on the table. "There aren't many. Once Dad left, Mom lost the camera, or so she said." She removed the lid from the box and pulled out a picture of a laughing, smiling couple. "They looked so young here."

"That's their one and only wedding picture."

"They got married in their bathing suits?" Everis glanced at Shar.

"Mom said they went to the beach, met some guy who was a pastor, and he married them. We have Dad's name, but they were never officially married. Mom's last name is plain old Jones." Shar sat down next to him and dumped out the box.

Maybe thirty pictures portrayed a few years of a couple together, and most of those were baby pictures. "Here we go." Everis studied a photo of a good-looking man sitting on a ratty sofa. Two little girls sat next to him. In his hand was a cigarette. On the coffee table was an ashtray full of butts. "I bet we can find someone to enhance the photo to where we can see what kind of cigarettes he smoked."

"Our father is not The Silencer." Candy crossed her arms. "He was a cheating fool, but not a killer. I'd swear on it."

"Well, someone connected to you and Shar is."

Chapter Nine

"I think we need to talk to your father." Everis glanced from Shar to Candy. "Either of you know where he is?"

Shar scooped up the photos. She needed to compose herself before letting loose the news that would cause her sister to explode. She'd rather face down a mean drunk than tell Candy she'd known where their father lived for the past three years. "In a trailer park, twenty miles away. It's just on the other side of the lake."

"When...why..." Candy's mouth opened and closed several times before she finally got the words out. "You've known for how long?"

"Three years." Shar gave a sheepish smile. "I haven't seen him. I've only looked up his address."

"Field trip." Everis stood. "Candy, I'm sorry you'll have to stay behind. This is part of our investigation, but if we find out he's not a threat to you, I'll make sure you get your father's address."

Her cheeks turned a bright red. "I'm not happy about it, but I understand. At least one of you has some compassion." She tossed the uneaten portion of her sandwich in the garbage and stormed to her car.

"I should have told her, but Candy knew our father way more than I did. She'd have gone straight out there to see him. If he wanted to see us, he would have found us." Shar set the photos back in the box and closed the lid. "I'm ready to go."

"Are you sure?" Everis peered into her face. "I can take Mayfield."

"No. This is my case, and the man is my father." Biologically, at least. "I'll do the unpleasant deed."

Everis's steady stare made her squirm. "You've convinced yourself that he's guilty before speaking with the man."

She stiffened. "Robert Camenetti is guilty of a lot of things, one of which may be murder." She refused to treat the man as anything other than a suspect. Candy could fawn over the man who fathered them, but Shar refused. She didn't have a father, hadn't had one in years, and she did just fine.

"Ok." Everis put his hands up and backed toward the door. "I'll follow your lead."

"Good." She pushed past him and marched to the jeep. She knew she was acting peevish, but Robert Camenetti was a sore subject.

They drove to the mobile home park in silence. Last year, Shar had made the drive alone and sat outside the faded green trailer for over an hour. She watched as Robert left, only to return half an hour later with a case of beer and something in a brown paper bag. He didn't go in the house, instead he sat in a worn lawn chair and popped beer after beer, littering the ground at his feet.

Just minutes before Shar left, a light blue sedan pulled to a stop next to him. A middle-aged woman with bright red hair that could only come from a cheap at-home application joined him in his drinking. Just one of a long line of women who saw something in Robert Camenetti.

Now, here she sat again, staring at the same dilapidated mobile home, watching the same still-handsome man drink himself to oblivion in the middle of the day. "There's the great Robert Camenetti."

In unison, she and Everis pushed open their doors and strolled up to him. Camenetti's eyes widened as he stared into Shar's face. "You look just like your mother did before she went to waste. What brings two cops to my door?"

"Could we step inside?" Everis asked. "I'd rather not question you where the entire park can hear."

"Oh, question me." Robert rose to his feet. "It's a disaster inside. I'm not much of a housekeeper, but I suppose you can clear off a couple of chairs. Just don't wake Dotty. She's a bear if she doesn't get her sleep."

"Would you rather come to the station?" Shar fought to keep her features impassive. "It would be more private."

"And have the world see my daughter haul me to the clink? Nah, we'll go inside."

She wanted to tell him she wasn't his daughter, but the words stuck in her throat.

Robert moved ahead of them, his right foot sinking into mud near the step. Size ten-and-a-half. Still, Shar couldn't envision a man that women flocked to killing them. Taking them to bed would be more his style.

The odor of stale cigarettes, beer, and spoiled food slammed her in the face as she stepped inside. Not much of a housekeeper was an understatement. Clothes and newspapers, paper plates and plastic cups littered every available surface and spilled onto the floor. Shar wrinkled her nose and swiped her arm across the sofa, knocking everything to the floor. She nodded for Everis to sit beside her.

Robert laughed and cleared off a chair facing them. "Now that we have that out of the way, how can I help my little girl?"

Shar exhaled long and slow. Be professional. Don't let him rattle you. "Are you aware of the serial killer stalking Highland Springs?"

He nodded, sliding a cigarette from a pack on top of a pile of magazines. "I'd ask if you mind, but this is my house." He fished a lighter from his shirt pocket and lit the Marlboro Red hanging from his lips. "Yeah, I saw the press conference. I tend to watch anything my girls are in."

Everis nudged Shar with his knee. The gesture kept her from blurting out how she felt about him calling her his girl.

"I need to know whether you recognize either of these women?" Shar handed him photographs of the victims.

"Only on the news." He barely glanced at the photos.

"Where are you employed, Mr. Camenetti?" Everis leaned forward, his gaze intent on Robert's face.

"I bartend at Harvey's." A run-down bar at the edge of Possum Ridge.

"Sir, we need to search your home. You can either cooperate or we can get a search warrant. Cooperation is the best thing for you."

He waved a hand and stubbed out the cigarette in a nearby ashtray. "Go ahead. I've nothing to hide. Just watch out for Dotty." He grinned, revealing still-white, still-straight teeth that looked as if he'd just had them bleached at the dentist's office.

Everis headed down the hall, leaving the kitchen/living area for Shar. She stood and rummaged through the pile of clothes and garbage on the end table.

"What exactly are you looking for?"

Without glancing up, Shar said, "Do you own a computer?"

"Who doesn't in this day and age?" He pulled one from under clothes. "You're doing a good job as Sheriff, Sharlene. I'm right proud of you."

"Look. You're Robert Camenetti. I'm Sheriff Camenetti. We share nothing but blood and a last name. Let's leave it at that."

"You're still sore at me for leaving your mother." He sighed and shook his head. "We were like oil and fire, igniting each other into fiery rages. It was best that we split."

"For us girls, I suppose." Shar opened the laptop. "Password."

"SharandCandy, no spaces."

Her gut wrenched. "You don't belong on social media?" The password didn't work. She knew for a fact he had an account.

"Of course, I do. Dotty must have changed it again. It bothers her that I use your names and not the kids we had together."

Her head jerked up. "Another sibling?"

He laughed. "Sweetheart, you've several. Everyone wants to have a piece of Robert Camenetti."

* * *

Everis closed his eyes at Camenetti's words, suspecting how much they wounded Shar. Regardless of how she acted as if the man didn't matter to her, he was her father. Add in the fact that they had three strikes against him with the size of his shoe, the brand of cigarettes he smoked, and the changed password on his computer, and Shar had to be ice cold inside.

"Hello, handsome." A bleached-blond woman leaned against the doorjamb to the bedroom. "Are those handcuffs hanging on your belt for me." She winked and grinned, revealing scarlet lipstick-stained teeth. Her soft stomach hung slightly over the thong she wore under a short tank top.

"No, ma'am. I would like to ask you a few questions, though."

"Fire away, dear."

"Do you live here?"

"Most of the time. Unless my no-good son needs me."

He pulled a pad from the inside pocket of his jacket. "Your name."

"Dorothy Winard, but everyone calls me Dotty."

"Occupation?"

"I dance on a pole at Harvey's." She took a step closer. "You could be a bit friendlier, gorgeous."

"Keep your distance, please." He speared her a sharp glance. "Does Mr. Camenetti leave for long periods of time?"

She laughed. "Of course, he does. He bartends. If they call him, he goes."

"I don't suppose you have his work schedule?"

"It's on the calendar in the kitchen."

"Thank you for your help." Everis turned and marched to a calendar on the kitchen wall that depicted half-naked girls sprawled across the hood of cars. He flipped through the pages, noting the dates Camenetti was scheduled to work. On the dates of the murders, he hadn't worked.

Everis unclipped the handcuffs from his belt. "Mr. Camenetti, we're arresting you on the suspicion of murder. You have the right to remain…"

"Call Bill, Dotty. Tell him I'm going to need his legal advice." Camenetti turned around, putting his hands behind his back. "Sharlene, you can't possibly believe your old man is a killer."

"The evidence states otherwise, sir." Back straight, she took hold of one arm, while Everis did the other.

"Watch your step," Everis told him as they led him down the steps.

"I'm not a killer."

"You'll have your opportunity to prove your innocence. Watch your head." Everis put his hand on the top of the man's head and assisted him into the backseat of Shar's jeep.

"Nice car," he said.

Shar rolled her eyes and climbed into the driver's seat. "This is why we need squad cars. So those in the back can't rattle on."

"You're as cold as a dead fish. Just like your mother."

Everis glared over the backseat. "Close your mouth, or I'll close it for you, sir."

Camenetti cackled. "That's right. Don't forget that *sir*, or I might have to accuse you of being downright disrespectful."

Everis clenched his fist and counted to ten. He hoped Camenetti was The Silencer. He really wanted to lock him up for the rest of his slimy life.

Back at the precinct, after swabbing Camenetti's mouth for his DNA, they put him into a holding cell and waited for the man's lawyer, if that's who Bill was, to arrive. Everis sat across from Shar and propped his feet on her desk. His gaze rested on her makeup-free face as she typed on her computer. "You alright?"

She nodded. "Never better."

"Don't shut me out. We're partners, remember."

"For the time being." She pushed her chair back and met his gaze with a tortured one. "No, I'm not okay. To find out that the man who sired me might be a serial killer is enough to tilt anyone's world."

"I agree." His cell phone rang. "Agent Hayes."

"We've got the results back on that DNA you asked us to put a rush on. I'm sending the results to the sheriff's department now."

"Thank you." He pressed off and grinned at Shar. "We've got the DNA. If we match your father to the cigarettes left at the scene, we'll have caught our man."

"The Silencer isn't my father." She turned her laptop. "That person is writing to me right now."

Chapter Ten

Shar focused her eyes back on the computer screen. Relief that the killer wasn't her father mingled with despair that they were still searching.

What do you do for a living?

I'm a receptionist.

Do you like it?

Sometimes. It's pretty boring otherwise. Small town, small life.

We'll have to get together sometime to brighten things up.

"Wow. This guy moves fast. He's already wanting to meet." Shar kept typing.

Maybe when I know you better. A girl can't be too careful nowadays.

This is good for now.

Phone's ringing. Bye.

Shar clicked out of the social media account. "I don't want to spend too much time talking to him. If it's someone who knows me, they'll pick up on that."

"I agree. So what do we do about Camenetti?"

"Let him go. We've nothing to hold him on. Will they put another rush on his DNA?" If he had kids scattered across Arkansas, chances were one of them could be The Silencer. Shar could possibly still share blood with a killer.

She stood from her chair. "I'll release him now."

Everis shot out his hand and stopped her with a touch on the arm. "We will catch him, Shar."

"You keep saying that." She gave him a shaky smile and headed for the holding cell. "You're free." She unlocked the door and held it open.

"I knew you'd come around." He held out his hands for her to remove the cuffs. "We should have dinner sometime and get reacquainted."

"Not much chance of that. Have a good day." She whirled and marched back to her office, slamming the door so he couldn't follow. Let him find his own way out.

"That was fast." Everis fixed his dark gaze on her again.

Why did his simple glance make her want to squirm like a five-year-old in church? His gaze bore through her as if he could see to her soul. "No reason to linger." She opened her top drawer and pulled out a notepad. "I could use the computer, but I think better with pencil and paper.

"We have The Silencer's shoe size, his DNA, the brand of cigarettes he smokes, and the fact he's probably a long-lost sibling of mine." She sneered. "Unless we get every man in Highland Springs to agree to a DNA test, we'll never match the DNA on the cigarettes."

Her computer dinged, signaling an email. She glanced at the screen. One from the lab and one from an unrecognized source. She opened the email. "Listen to this, Everis. You're getting closer, dear sheriff. Isn't this fun?"

"He knows we brought Camenetti in. We need to

talk some more with your father." He jumped up from his chair and raced out of her office.

Shar stayed close on his heels, stopping short at the sight of her father flirting with Natalie. "Robert, a word, please."

He sighed dramatically. "My daughter once again beckons me. It was nice meeting you, Miss Natalie."

Natalie peered around him at Shar and raised her eyebrows. "This is your father?"

With a sharp nod, she ushered Robert into her office. She handed him a pencil and a fresh notepad. "Write down the names of all my siblings. If you can't remember them, write down their mother's name."

"This might take a while." He winked and sat down. "Not to be crude, but I've been busy since your mother kicked me out."

"Because you cheated."

He shrugged. "Some men just can't be tied down. Ain't that right, Agent?"

To his credit, Everis didn't respond. Instead, he stood against the wall, arms crossed, a stoic expression on his handsome face.

Shar resumed her seat behind her desk and forwarded the email to IT in Little Rock. She didn't hold out much hope they could trace the sender.

Robert slid the paper across her desk. "Quite the list. I'm a bit ashamed."

Five brothers and three sisters, not counting Candy. "You're a sick man. I suggest counseling."

"You aren't the first." He stood. "I'm serious about dinner sometime. Tell your sister to come see me before we're both too old." He gave a wheezing laugh. "I turn sixty tomorrow."

"Don't expect a cake or a card." Shar didn't get up. Shock glued her to her seat. She knew the names listed, and probably knew the ones with question marks next to their names. Highland Springs and the surrounding small towns didn't have a large population.

She glanced at the clock. "Quitting time. Let's grab supper and then ask Candy if she's familiar with any of these people. One of them is our killer. I feel it in my gut."

* * *

The Silencer felt a tremor of nervousness at how close the sheriff got to him. She'd figured out the old man. Of course, she was smart. He knew that. Her figuring out the clues did not surprise him. What did scare him was the fierce-eyed agent that accompanied the sheriff everywhere. Why couldn't it be the dunderhead Mayfield that went around with her?

He started his car and pulled out of the sheriff's office parking lot a few seconds after the sheriff and Agent Hayes did. They turned right in the direction of Main Street. He followed.

When they drove through a fast-food drive-thru, he let one car in between them, then did the same. Following her, eating the same foods, made him feel closer to her than anything else could.

He pulled up to place his order. "What did the people in the black jeep order?"

"Two chicken strip meals," a bored-sounding young man said.

"I'll take the same, except one order, please. Same kind of sauce and soda."

"Diet or regular?"

"Diet." Shar would stick to regular, he was sure.

When the sheriff and her tagalong drove from the restaurant to her house, The Silencer continued past to his own home half a mile away. He had some courting to do. Unfortunately, the new gal wasn't online much. Her social media presence was spotty at best. He'd need to woo someone else in the meantime.

Behind the closed curtains of his modest two-bedroom farmhouse, he set his supper on a glass plate, poured the soda into a glass, and booted up his computer. He typed in Highland Springs and browsed the faces that came up.

The new receptionist for the police department looked promising...oh, wait. That's the woman keeping him at arm's length. It would be wonderful to snatch her right under the agent's nose. Risky, too.

He continued the hunt, finally settling on the waitress from the Western bar and restaurant. Wait. No, he couldn't take a woman with a child. That would make him no better than his mother.

He bit into a chicken tender. Not bad for fast food, although it wouldn't do a thing for his waistline. He continued searching, finally spotting the perfect target. A lovely redhead by the name of Linda. He wouldn't bother wooing her. It said here she liked to jog. That made her an easy target. Leaving traces of himself on social media only increased his chances of being caught.

It appeared The Silencer was going to start jogging in the morning. He grinned and closed his laptop.

Candy stared at the list. "These are all our half-siblings?"

"So he says." Shar made them all a drink and joined

Everis and her sister at the table.

"Shar seems to think one of these men are The Silencer."

"But Mark works at the post office. Ben delivers water. They aren't violent." She shook her head. "No, it would have to be one of the question marks. Ben and Mark are just as clueless as we are about being related." She put a hand over her stomach. "I made out with Mark. I think I'm going to be sick."

"Stop being dramatic." Shar slid the list back in front of her. "You didn't know. Is our brother a good kisser?" Her eyes sparkled.

Everis laughed, happy to see some of the weight of the day slip from her shoulders. "My brother and I joke with each other all the time. I miss him, but he's an airline pilot. I rarely see him."

"You'll have to experience sibling rivalry voraciously through us." Shar smiled, sending his heart into a nosedive. He wanted to kiss her. Bad. It was a very good thing that her sister was there, or he'd embarrass himself and probably get shot for his troubles.

"How do we go about finding out who the other three are?" Candy downed her cosmo like a dying woman and got up to make another. "Seriously. Other than you taking the DNA of every man in town…"

"We question the mothers first." Shar twirled her drink on a napkin.

"There's also the fact your father may not have listed everyone," Everis said. He hated the looks of disappointment on the women's faces. "He lives in a beer fog."

"He lives in a dump," Shar spit.

"Well, I'm still going to get to know him." Candy shot her sister a defiant look. "He's the only father we have."

"Best not to have one if he's it."

Everis needed to steer the conversation to safer waters. Fast. "We'll research these women first thing in the morning, then approach them at their home or work. We're getting closer, ladies."

"How do you stay so optimistic?" Shar rolled her eyes, all traces of the sheriff gone, replaced by a beautiful, but irritated woman. "We're dealing with a sick-o. A man who tortures women in brutal ways and films it. Yet, you're always...so...optimistic."

"What purpose does it serve to be otherwise?"

"I'm going to bed. Let me know when you found out which of our darling brothers is a killer." Candy huffed off.

When she'd left, Everis continued. "I could be hardened and pessimistic, but that would only hurt me. I lived for a time heading home to a bottle every night. Not just a beer or two. I'm talking the hard stuff. When my brother came to visit and found me drunk with a loaded gun beside me—he had my young nephew with him—it was a wake-up call. It was either change my way of looking at things or die. I chose life."

Her light-colored gaze never left his face as he talked. Her features were as smooth and impassive as when she questioned a suspect or lectured a wayward teen. Only a flicker of sympathy in her eyes told him how she felt.

"I'm sorry you went through that."

"How do you keep yourself sane?"

She took her bottom lip between her teeth, making

it harder for him to keep a few feet between them. She blinked a few times, then said, "I'm here for the people of this town. As long as they need me, I have purpose."

"Why isn't there a man in your life?"

She ducked her head. "I don't have time. No man wants a woman who can be called out of bed at any time or during a romantic dinner."

"Some men don't mind. I dated for a while. She left me for the very reason you mentioned. Maybe you just need to find a man with the same demands on him as you have."

She laughed and refilled her drink at the kitchen counter. "Are you vying for the job?"

He rose and stood so close behind her that his breath ruffled her hair. He took the silky strands in his hands and brushed them to one side. "Would you mind if I were?" He lowered his head, resting his lips gently on her neck.

She gave a small gasp that fueled his blood.

He turned her around in his arms and buried his hands in her hair, tilting her face to his. When she didn't protest, ensnaring him with her crystal eyes, he claimed her lips in a kiss. Soft, gentle, with slowly increasing pressure until her arms found their way around his neck.

She tasted like lime and cranberry. She smelled like...Shar. Flowery and something fruity. Fresh.

Moving forward, he pressed her against the counter, lifting her until she sat on the edge, never releasing her lips. His hands untangled from her hair and slid down her back. He came up for air and buried his face in her neck. "Good night, Shar. If I stay, we'll take a step we can't get back." He straightened and placed his lips against her forehead. "Sweet dreams, beautiful."

His feet pivoted and he walked out the door. One of the hardest things he'd ever had to do.

Chapter Eleven

After a restless night, Shar woke and stared at the ceiling. What right died Everis have in determining what she'd regret and wouldn't. Yes, she would have regretted a night of passion without love or commitment, but his kiss had felt too good to be true. She really needed to do something about her lonely state before she did something foolish.

She swung her legs over the side of the bed and headed for the shower. How was she going to be able to work with Everis today without acting like a fool? Her face heated just thinking of their kiss. She prided herself on keeping her features impassive while working. Seeing him would be a true test to her skill.

An hour later, she shoved open the door to the coffee shop and froze. Everis leaned on his elbow on the counter, engaged in conversation with the barista who blushed and giggled. The man was definitely a charmer. And right after kissing Shar until her blood boiled. He was nothing but a flirt like every other good-looking man.

He spotted Shar. Still grinning, he waved her over. "I thought I'd treat you to coffee this morning. This lovely young woman was very helpful. She knows what everyone usually orders. Even Robert Camenetti." He waggled his eyebrows. "Why, I bet Clari here knows everyone in Highland Springs."

Clever man. He flirted to get information, using what the good Lord gave him in droves. Shar felt better and smiled. "Clari is a true asset to our town." In fact, the recent high school graduate probably did know a lot about everyone. "Are you active on social media, Clari?"

"Very. I spend hours on there talking to people." She took Everis's credit card and swiped it through the machine. "I've met the nicest guy."

Shar jerked her attention to Everis, then back to the girl. "Does he have a name?"

"Billy. Isn't that cute? He graduated from Harrison the same year I did."

Shar spun around and gave a sharp look to a man complaining about the slow-moving line. "It'll take longer, sir, if I question her away from the counter."

"Clari, we, the sheriff and I, would like you to do us a favor." Everis snared her gaze. "I want you to agree to meet this guy. Let us know the time and place. Do not meet him alone."

Her eyes widened. "You think he's the killer," she whispered.

"We aren't ruling anyone out. Will you do that for us?"

"I'll do it right now." She pulled her cell phone from the pocket of her apron and punched some buttons. "I bet I'll have an answer before your drinks are done."

"We'll wait right over here. You're a gem." Everis smiled.

Shar joined him at the end of the counter. "Very smooth, agent."

"Let's hope this works and we have a suspect in custody within a few hours."

"That would be awesome." Shar watched as Clari took orders from the customers and another young woman fixed their drinks. When Clari glanced at her phone and nodded in their direction, she knew they'd received an answer.

Clari joined them. "Tonight, at the library, eight o'clock."

Shar put her hand over the girl's. "Do not meet him outside. Make him go inside to get you. Understand?"

She nodded. "I'm scared."

"Chances are he is exactly who he says he is, but a girl can't be too careful. Don't tell anyone, Clari. Not even your best friend. We'll see you tonight."

Everis grabbed the carrier of drinks. "I walked, so if you don't mind, I'll catch a ride with you rather than carry these drinks back."

"That's fine." She relaxed at his attitude, as if nothing happened the night before. Maybe she had dwelled on the kiss too long. Lots of people kissed, right? The kind that made your heart pound and your pulse race, right? Everis would head back to Little Rock once the case was finished. She shouldn't dwell on anything with him for too long.

He reached over and touched her hand, making her forget everything she'd just decided. "I enjoyed last night."

"Oh. Yeah. It was nice." For crying out loud. She steered into traffic and toward the station.

"Nice?" He chuckled. "Yeah, you could say that."

Shar parked in her designated spot and held the drinks while Everis exited the jeep and came to the driver's side. He took them from her, his gaze meeting hers with a tenderness that left her speechless.

"Are we still visiting the mothers of your brothers?"

"What?" His question brought her back to earth. "Oh, yes. As soon as I go through emails and snail mail." She grabbed her drink from the carrier and headed to her office. When Mayfield walked by, she called his name. "Sit, please, and tell me Amber is fine."

He sat across from her desk. "That girl is high maintenance, but yeah, she's safe. She wanted the most expensive resort, a suite, and a mini-fridge full of tiny bottles of champagne and chocolate. She had to settle for a three star with free WiFi. Wasn't happy." He took a sip from his drink. "Nice of Everis. Anyway, then she proceeded to complain about the Ford Fusion I rented for her. You just can't make some people happy."

Shar grinned. "No, you can't. I appreciate you undertaking that task. Agent Hayes and I will be questioning three women who may know more about The Silencer today, so—"

"You mean women that did the under-the-sheet Tango with your old man." He smiled.

"Don't spread that around." She booted up her computer, flirted a bit more with the mystery man wanting to kill, uh, meet her…not every man was a killer. "Then, this evening we're headed to the library to set a trap. I'd like for you to be there."

"Sure thing, boss. Right now, I've a stack of messages on my desk to respond to. Oh, and the new receptionist is hot." He wiggled his eyebrows and exited her office.

Shar's smile widened. Mark was always good for a

laugh. She scrolled through her emails, deleted most of them, responded to the few that needed an answer, then sorted through the mail piled on top of her in-basket. Toward the bottom was a letter with her father's address. Why would he send her a letter after she'd seen him the day before?

Using a sharp letter opener, she slit the envelope open and pulled out a sheet of copy paper.

"Dear Sheriff,

You found the old man. Very good. I'm sure he was full of useless information. The new receptionist is very lovely. I look forward to meeting her.

The Silencer."

Shar pressed her lips together and rang for Natalie to step into her office. "Forward the calls here." She slid the letter across her desk.

Natalie read the letter, then glanced up, a serious look in her dark eyes. "Looks like I've got a fan. I think this means I've met this guy. I'll go try and set up a meeting and have Clari cancel hers."

"Let's run through the list of men you've met while you've been here." Everis stepped into the room, having caught Natalie's statement. He took a glance at the letter, then perched on the edge of Shar's desk.

"I'm not sure I can remember them all," Natalie said. "I'm sure I haven't spoken with every man who knows I'm the receptionist now."

Using two fingers, Shar pushed a notepad across the desk. Lying on top was a ball point pen. "As many names as possible."

She sat in the one free chair in the room. "The guy who delivers the water, what's his name...Mark Arnes?

Ben Wilson delivers the mail to me personally instead of putting it in the box outside. Jack Leroy fills the vending machine. I guess I can add the landlord where I'm renting, but the man is seventy something."

"I doubt he's our man." Everis motioned for her to continue.

"Seriously, Ev, I've met most men in this town in one way or the other by making myself visible, not to mention how many people come in this office. Lars Townsend, the reporter, Mark Mayfield, the deputy, that drunk man who stumbles in here once a week. Ted something."

"Keep your wits about you, Nat. The Silencer is on the prowl and may have you as his next target."

"I don't go anywhere without my gun or my pepper spray." She stood. "I'll watch every man who gives me more than a passing glance a bit deeper. If anyone triggers anything, I'll let you know."

"Thanks." Everis took the chair she vacated. "I made the calls to the three women whose sons we don't have names for. I left two messages, and one said we could stop by between six and seven."

"I guess we'll talk to her before heading to the library." Shar studied the names on the list. "I know every one of these men. Some have been around my whole life."

"Who moved here around the time Arnett would have been killed?"

While she thought, her gaze fixed on a spot on the wall, Everis took the opportunity to study her. Like traitors, his thoughts and gaze went straight to her lips and how full and soft they'd felt. He longed to kiss her again and again. He wanted to hear the little catch she made in her throat when she submitted to the feelings racing through them both.

"Everis?"

"Sorry. I was off somewhere more pleasant." He left his gaze on her lips, smiling when she pressed them together and ducked her head.

"Lars is fairly new to town, but he arrived last year. Mark moved here about six months ago, which," she chuckled, "is when he must have kissed his sister. She likes to make a move on any new guy."

"Don't say kissed."

She jerked up. Her beautiful mouth opened, then closed before the mask she liked to wear fell into place. "I wondered when you were going to bring that up."

"I don't regret the kiss, Shar. I enjoyed it very much. In fact, I intend to have another, then maybe another one after that. What do you say?"

She narrowed her eyes. "Not here."

"Of course, not here. Stop talking about things irrelevant to the case while we're working."

"Okay, but I'll still be thinking about kissing you during our down time. I like the way talking about it makes your cheeks turn as pink as one of those pencil erasers. Remember those?" His mouth twitched.

"Stop it, Everis." She slapped the notepad. "You're being unprofessional."

"In what way?"

"You're...you're...causing me not to act like a sheriff."

"You mean, I'm making you feel like a desirable woman? How long since you've felt that way, Shar?" He tilted his head. "Can't you be a woman and a sheriff? I haven't known you long, but I've seen how soft you are, how much you love the people of this town, how fair you are with them. Why put on a hard mask while doing those things?"

Her gaze had remained locked on his face as he spoke. "I want people to take me seriously. This killer wouldn't have picked my town if he didn't think he could win."

"A killer doesn't usually pick a town because of the sheriff unless he has a vendetta against that sheriff. Which this guy seems to have. What we need to do is find out why he's targeted you and Highland Springs. It has nothing to do with your ability. It's all about the final showdown." He leaned forward. "Which we will win."

Chapter Twelve

Morning his foot. It was after lunch before his target jogged toward his hiding place. The Silencer stepped from the bushes and sat on the side of the trail pretending to nurse a sore ankle.

"Good morning." The woman stopped, jogging in place beside him, parts of her body bouncing pleasantly. Someday he really should find a lovely woman and settle down.

No alarm showed in her hazel eyes. Why should it? His face was well known around town. "Do you need help?"

"Unfortunately, I'm new to the act of jogging and failed to veer around a rock. I've twisted my ankle." He grimaced.

"Let me help you to your car."

"But, that will interrupt your run."

She smiled. "It's my second time around. I'm rather obsessed. It won't hurt me to stop and help a fellow man."

"Then I gratefully accept your help."

With her assistance, he limped by her side to his car. When she turned to go, he quickly jabbed her neck with a hypodermic needle and caught her as she crumbled. He laid her in the backseat of his car, checked to make sure she had her cellphone tucked into her exercise belt, and sped to the other side of the lake. He knew just the spot on the edge of town where they could have privacy. No one would hear her scream but the birds.

*   *
*

"Still haven't heard back from the two women I left a message with," Everis said, sliding into the passenger seat of the jeep. "Do you want to stop by their residence?"

"If we have time. We need to visit with Mrs. Mayne, Mark Arnes's mother, then get to the library before Natalie." Shar caught a glimpse of a teen boy with a spray can of paint and made a sharp right.

Pulling up beside him, she rolled down the passenger window. "Hey, Jason. What's up?"

He startled, trying to hide the can behind his back. "Uh, headed to help my dad."

"At the pharmacy? That's nice of you. What's the paint for?"

Everis turned to the side, trying to hide a grin, which didn't help Shar keep a smile off her lips. She wiggled her fingers. "Hand it over."

The strong smell of paint fumes drifted through the open window. "Where have you tagged?"

"Nowhere." He handed the can to Everis.

Shar narrowed her eyes. "If I see any sign of red spray paint where it shouldn't be, I'm knocking on your door."

"Fine. I tagged the wall by the junkyard."

"Get in."

Everis glanced over. "Do we have time for this?"

"We'll have to make time. I believe in addressing

the issue right off, and this young man has some paint to clean off a wall." Once Jason was sitting sullen in the backseat, Shar switched directions and parked next to a wooden fence with curse words sprayed across the planks. "Not very creative, Jason." Shar turned off the engine and moved to the back. She pulled out a can of turpentine and a bundle of rags. "Get busy. We're on a time crunch."

Sighing, Jason took the supplies and scrubbed the wall, muttering the very words he worked at wiping off.

A scream ripped the air. Shar's hand went for her weapon. She froze, straining to hear which direction the sound came from.

"This way." Everis scaled the fence.

"Give me a boost, Jason. Don't go anywhere. Get in the jeep and lock the doors."

He folded his hands into a stirrup, hoisting her up, then dashed for the jeep as another scream sounded that chilled Shar's blood. She caught sight of Everis disappearing around a rusty truck. He appeared to be heading to the opposite side of the junkyard.

When Shar caught up with him, he hunkered behind a pile of crushed cars. He put a finger to his lip and pointed toward a broken-down school bus. Another scream, cut off midway, a rattle and a thump, then the sound of pounding feet.

"I'll go after the runner, you check in the bus." Everis sprinted away, gun at the ready.

Shar darted up the steps of the bus and stopped short. A woman's legs dangled over a tattered seat. Propped against a carburetor on the opposite seat was a cell phone recording the woman's death. Blood pooled from the slit in her throat. She gurgled.

Shar knelt beside her and pressed her hands against the woman's throat. "Hold on. We'll get help." She pressed the button on her radio and called for an ambulance. They'd be too late, but any hope she could give the woman was better than none. She kept her gaze locked on the woman's eyes until the light faded from them.

Tears blurred her own. They'd come so close to getting there in time to prevent her death.

Footsteps sounded behind her. Shar whipped out her Ruger and whirled. "I almost shot you, Everis."

"I lost him in the woods. The woman?"

"She didn't make it. We weren't fast enough." Shar picked up a rag from the floor and did her best to wipe the blood from her hands and weapon. "Was it The Silencer?"

He shrugged. "I think so. At least the footprints match." He pounded the back of a seat. "So close!"

"I need to get back to Jason. I'll send him home and be right back." Shar hurried back to the jeep, surprised to see Lars talking to the boy. "I thought I told you to lock the door."

"I did," Jason said. "He knocked on the window. Wanted to know what I was doing here."

Shar transferred her attention to the reporter. "He was cleaning off the graffiti."

Lars grinned, out of breath. "He told me. Then, he said ya'll heard screams and you and the agent scaled the wall. What's going on?" He swiped his arm across his sweaty forehead. "You've blood on your hands and radio."

"Why do you look as if you've been running?"

"Because I have been. Can't you tell? I went

jogging."

He did look the part in sweat shorts, a tee shirt and a water bottle clipped to his belt. "I suppose you saw my jeep and just had to stop."

He grinned. "I've called my cameraman, too. There's a story here, I'm sure."

"Jason, go home. We'll finish up here another time, but I strongly suggest you call Mr. Berkemeyer and tell him what you did to his fence and that you'll take care of the damage. Understood?"

"Yes, ma'am." He slid from the backseat and raced away.

Shar grabbed a water bottle from the back of the jeep and washed the rest of the blood from her hands, then used a hand wipe to wipe down the radio. "Another woman was killed. I'll let you come with me if you promise to keep your distance. We don't need you contaminating the scene." She glanced up as his cameraman zoomed next to the jeep. "Same goes for him."

Everis scowled when he caught sight of the news reporter and cameraman following Shar. Rushing past them were the paramedics. Too late. He hadn't even caught a glimpse of the person fleeing the scene. If not for the cell phone recording, they couldn't be positive it was The Silencer.

"Why'd you bring the rats?"

Shar laughed. "Lars was jogging past, saw my jeep, and Jason blabbed. He wouldn't budge, so I told him to come along and stay out of the way."

The cameraman trained his lens on the school bus while Lars rattled on about the discovery of another body just minutes after the murder. Wonderful. He just had to add how the sheriff and her agent sidekick were just a little too late. Everis really disliked the press and their insatiable thirst for a story, any story.

He'd lost too many cases because of too much information being leaked to the public. "Make sure he doesn't give away too much." Everis kicked a can and shuffled away.

A disgruntled husband had shot his wife and child while a cameraman filmed the whole thing. The man had called the station saying he needed help. The news people arrived before the police were called. By then the woman was dead and the child in critical condition.

The bureau solved more cases than not, but every life lost was another win for the bad guys. Everis really wanted the scales to tip in the favor of Highland Springs with this case. The killer was moving too fast. His kills often and swift. And they were escalating. His gaze scanned the ground between the bus and the edge of the junkyard.

Spotting a pile of dog poop, he stopped. Where was the dog? He hadn't heard a bark when they pulled up. Junkyard dogs were known for their fierce territorial protectiveness.

He climbed in the bed of a rusty Nissan truck and scanned the yard. At the far end stood a tool shed. Everis jumped to the ground and hurried in that direction.

Sure enough, a doghouse, a food dish and a water bowl sat outside the shed. Everis pushed open the door and caught sight of a very groggy mixed-breed dog. He squatted next to the animal. "Someone sent you to La-La land, didn't they, boy?" He clipped a nearby leash onto the dog's collar and led him to Shar.

"What's that?"

"A very high junkyard dog. He needs to go to the vet when we're finished here. Where's the owner?"

"In the hospital recuperating from heart surgery. He has a high school kid keeping an eye on the place and the dog after school." Shar shook her head. "Too many people involved in this ever-increasing web."

"Whoever killed the woman knew the junkyard layout. Do we have her ID yet?"

"Her social media page says her name is Allie Moore, twenty-eight, elementary school teacher. I'm enforcing a curfew and issuing another warning to the women of this town. From her clothes, Allie had been jogging." The hard mask she reserved for work slipped into place. She turned and marched toward the reporter, Everis close on her heels.

"Turn off the camera."

"Why?" Lars lowered his microphone. "The town deserves to know what's going on here."

"Because I'm going to ask you some question that you may not want on film," Everis said, lowering the camera.

Lars looked annoyed, but told his coworker to turn off the camera. "We were filming live."

"The station will cover for you. The victim was dressed for jogging." Everis scanned Lar's outfit. "You're dressed for jogging. Did you see her?"

He shook his head. "There are plenty of places to jog around here, agent. The lake, the sidewalks, the track around the football field. It's rare I see the same person twice."

"It seems strange to me that you'd be jogging at this

time on a weekday."

"I'm freelance. My hours are whatever I want them to be. Do you mind? If you aren't arresting me on suspicion of murder, then I have work to do before I call it a day."

Everis blew air sharply out his nose as the camera was turned back on and trained on the body bag on the gurney as the paramedics wheeled Allie Moore away.

Shar stood next to him. "Every man in Highland Springs is a suspect at this point. Especially if they wear a size 10 ½ gym shoe." She pointed to Lar's feet. "He fits the build."

"Same tread, too."

"Look." Lars had the camera turned off again. "I'm trying to film live, and you're making me out to be a suspect. These shoes are very popular and can be bought at any outlet mall in the country."

"You're still going on the suspect list," Shar said. "So is your cameraman. Luke Ball, right?"

The man nodded, face grim.

Everis grinned. He loved it when Shar played tough. "Have a good evening, gentlemen." Keeping a tight hold on the dog's leash, he followed Shar back to the jeep.

Chapter Thirteen

"I'm very sorry we're late," Shar told the frazzled woman. They'd arrived at Mrs. Mayne's house at six-thirty. "Please forgive us. We'll make this as short as possible." Especially since she wanted to be at the library well before Natalie showed up.

"Come in, but I really don't have much time. My husband will be home, and I've got to get his supper on before I go to work." She stepped back and held the door open. "I'll tell you right now I ain't seen that no good Camenetti in years. No offense, Sheriff."

"None taken."

Mrs. Mayne motioned for them to sit at the kitchen table. "I'll cook, you talk."

Hopefully, the woman would join in the conversation. Shar folded her hands on a dinette set straight out of *Leave It to Beaver*. "I understand you had a child with Mr. Camenetti."

"Yes, a boy. The joy of my heart. I'm so proud of Mark. He delivers mail, you know."

Which gave him privy to a lot of town secrets and vulnerable women. "You're sure Camenetti is the father?"

The woman spun. One hand gripped a knife. "What kind of woman do you take me for?"

Everis nudged Shar's leg with his knee. "We're

sorry, ma'am, but with a killer running loose, we sometimes have to ask uncomfortable questions." He smiled.

The woman immediately relaxed, sucked in to his charm like every other woman who breathed. "I'm just a little on edge. I spend a lot of time alone."

"What does your husband do, ma'am?" Shar kept her features impassive.

"He works at the post office in Eureka Springs. He's the one who got Mark on here." She banged a pan on the stove. "It's obvious Mark ain't his biological son, but he don't know who the real father is, and I'd prefer it kept that way."

"Why?" Everis glanced up from taking notes.

"They don't like each other 'cause of something that happened in high school."

"Ma'am." Shar squared her shoulders. "If we have to dig every piece of information out of you, this is going to take all night."

"I never took you for such a bossy person before, Sheriff." She slammed a lid on the pan. "They fought over the same gal in high school. Your slutty mother, if you want the truth. Now, do you understand why my Will won't want to know he's got Camenetti's leftovers?"

Shar understood. She also saw a motive for murdering women if Mr. Mayne held a resentment toward the fairer sex. Obviously Everis thought the same, since he wrote the man's name on the pad.

Shar stood. "Ma'am, we'll need a sample of your husband's DNA. We're taking it from every man we come across. Doesn't mean anything. We're just ruling out the innocent." Which reminded her she needed to stop and get Lars's and his cameraman's samples.

"Well, that's the garage door, so you can get it now. Good luck with that."

Mr. Mayne, a big, burly man, scowled as he entered the kitchen. "What's going on here?"

"We're collecting DNA from the men of Highland Springs, sir." Shar forced a smile. "We're hoping you'll cooperate to show your innocence."

He cut a glance at his wife, who nodded. "I reckon that's alright."

"Please, come to the station at your earliest convenience. Tomorrow would be best." Shar handed him her business card. "Thank you for your cooperation. Please have Mark stop by, too."

Mrs. Mayne followed them to the door. "Please don't tell Mark who his father is. He doesn't know anything."

"That's not very fair, is it?" Shar stepped onto the porch. "Not many people would regret being my sibling."

"It ain't you, it's your father." She slammed the door.

"That went well." She marched to the jeep and climbed into the driver's seat.

"As well as can be expected." Everis joined her inside. "Mark will find out before this is through. The woman will have to deal with the aftermath."

Shar turned the key in the ignition. "Not my problem." She didn't mean to be callous, but the wreckage from her father's infidelities was mounting. Soon, she'd drown beneath their weight.

The junkyard dog hung his massive head over the seat and drooled on her shoulder. "That's a mastiff," she told Everis. "Or at least part. I'm guess the other is big baby." She shoved the dog's head back.

"He knows a pretty woman when he sees one."

Her face heated as she drove toward town. She liked the dog. Maybe she should get one. Maybe Mr. Berkemeyer would sell this one. She glanced in the rearview mirror. The dog sat tall on the seat, staring straight ahead. She smiled and took the backway to the library.

Once there, she parked behind a thick stand of trees. She left the window open and told the dog to stay. Together, she and Everis entered the library through the backdoor.

"I'd prefer that the authorities enter through the front like everyone else." A woman who appeared to be in her fifties, stern and ramrod straight, marched toward them. "As the librarian, I expect rules to be followed."

"The former librarian didn't seem to mind when we were on an investigation," Shar said. She glanced at the woman's name tag. Who wore name tags anymore? "Sorry for the inconvenience, Ms. Mansfield. We'll remember next time."

The woman narrowed her eyes, refusing to break eye contact with Everis. Impressive.

They moved through the library, with a nod toward Natalie, who stood in the foyer, then took up position in the alcove next to the restrooms. Now they waited.

※ ※ ※

The Silencer pulled in front of the library and eyed the massive dog sitting on the steps. He'd seen that dog somewhere before. He climbed the stairs, keeping several feet between him and the dog. "Hello, boy."

The dog kept its gaze locked on The Silencer as he

reached for the door. The agent. This was the dog from the junkyard.

The Silencer took a few steps backward. Was it a trap? Was the lovely Natalie a spy for the sheriff? She was the receptionist there. Had she mentioned she would meet with him? He swiveled and ran back to his car. The night wouldn't be a waste. He just needed a new plan.

* * *

"He should have been here half an hour ago." Nat's voice drifted through Everis's earpiece. "The librarian is scowling at me. I have to admit the women scares me."

"I don't think he's coming," Everis said. "He somehow got wind we'd be here."

"Why is there a giant of a dog staring through the library door?" Mrs. Mansfield stepped into the alcove and crossed her arms. "Does he belong to you?"

"How the hell did he get out of the jeep?" Everis shook his head. "The dog gave us away. The Silencer had to have recognized him."

"The library is closing. Please leave." The librarian marched away.

"She might very well be scarier than The Silencer." Shar headed for the door.

Everis joined her. The dog was huge, beautiful, and might very well have set them back in their investigation. "How did you get your lug of a body through the jeep window?"

"Sheer determination," Shar said, scratching the animal between the ears. "I wonder what his name is. He looks like a Goliath to me."

The dog tilted his head and stared at her. "Goliath, it

is." The dog followed them to the jeep.

"That sucks." Shar planted her fists on her hips. "Where's the window?"

Everis grinned and peered into the frame where the window should be. "It looks to me as if he shoved it all the way down trying to get out."

Goliath looked behind them, his ears up.

"I'm headed home," Nat said, through her voice piece. "See you two in the morning. Wait. There's a car parked in the shadows. I can see the gleam of a cigarette."

"Get in your car and lock the door." Everis raced for the parking lot, Goliath and Shar at his side.

A car roared away as they approached. The driver flicked his cigarette out the window

"Not again." Everis aimed his weapon at the rear tire and squeezed the trigger.

He missed, and the car disappeared around the corner. His shoulders slumped and he had the distinct desire to punch something, drink something, anything to help erase the disappointment of The Silencer escaping again. All Everis had seen was that the vehicle was a dark sedan. Still, he called and put out an APB on a car fitting that description, then glared at the dog.

"Goliath, if you interfere with our investigation again, I'm arresting you." He stormed back to the jeep and waited for the dog and Shar to join him.

"It's not the dog's fault." Shar opened the door to the backseat and let Goliath jump in. "He didn't want to be alone, is all."

"The Silencer may or may not have gotten out of his car. He may or may not have recognized the dog. What made him leave was seeing us. What led him to that is anyone's guess." Shar closed the door and climbed into the driver's seat.

"My educated guess is that he saw the dog." Everis slammed his door. He snagged the seatbelt hard enough to make it lock up. No amount of tugging was going to loosen it. He groaned and let go, then slowly clicked it into place.

"You need a drink, Mr. Agent Man." She drove them to her house. "I'm going to ask Mr. Berkemeyer if I can keep the dog."

"You're serious."

"I am. I like him." She flashed a sideways grin, exited the jeep, and let Goliath out. The dog trotted next to her like a small horse.

Everis shook his head and followed. He'd been replaced by a dog, before having a chance at a relationship with Shar.

"Make yourself comfortable," she called from the kitchen. "I'm calling the hospital."

When she set her mind to something, nothing could stop her. Everis sat on the sofa and longed for a beer and a pizza. "When you're done with the dog, could you please order a pizza? Failure makes me hungry."

She peered around the corner. "What? Not feeling your motto of 'we'll catch him right now'?"

"Nope." He feared they might not. The killer would kill until his satiation with Highland Springs was done, then move on to fresh pastures. The world held an unending number of young women who posted their lives on social media.

"The dog is mine. The owner is selling the junkyard and moving away." Shar plopped down next to him. "His name really is Goliath. He's eating a leftover chicken breast right now." She hugged a pillow to her chest. "He's beautiful."

Everis twisted his mouth. "Pizza?"

"Oh, I forgot." She reached for her pocket.

"Never mind. I'll call." He pulled his from inside his jacket and ordered a large Mega Meat. Then, he called the local pet store that delivered, and ordered their largest bag of dog food. "You can't feed him people food. It isn't healthy for him."

"You do like him." She playfully bumped him with her shoulder. "Why don't you find something on television to watch while I change out of my uniform?"

Everis nodded and shrugged out of his jacket. "Nothing but an action flick with explosions."

"Sounds good." She returned five minutes later in short shorts and a tee shirt that reached almost to where the shorts stopped.

Everis's mouth dried up. How could she look so good when she dressed ratty? "Uh, I found an old one. Movie. Yeah."

She handed him a beer. "I think you could use this."

"Thanks." He downed half of it in one gulp.

Goliath stared at the front door and growled low in his throat.

"Pizza already?" Shar asked.

"Can't be." Everis grabbed the gun he'd set on the coffee table. "Get back." He moved to the window and parted the curtains just far enough to peer out. A sheet of paper flapped from the porch post.

Chapter Fourteen

"**Don't tell me to get back.**" Shar stepped next to him and peeked over his shoulder. "I'm the sheriff, not a hapless victim."

Retrieving her Ruger from the foyer side table, she opened the front door and scanned the yard. Not seeing anyone, she started to step outside when Goliath planted his body firmly in her path. Just as she noticed that the paper was actually stuck to the post with an arrow, another arrow whizzed past her head and lodged in the doorframe.

Shar stumbled backward, snatching the paper as she did, then slammed the door. "I don't think that's Robin Hood. Good boy." She patted Goliath's head. "You saved my life."

Everis looked at the note. The scent of him sent her heart racing. They really needed to solve this case before she did something stupid. "Are you enjoying the game, sis?" she read. Okay, he's admitting they're related. Yay for Shar. She glanced up at Everis, bringing her face within kissing distance. She cleared her throat. "I need to find out what this man has against me." She stepped back. "And why he thinks he needs to kill because of it."

"He isn't killing because of you." Everis turned to the door as footsteps sounded on the porch. "I'm guessing that's the pizza." He opened the door just enough to take the pizza from the boy and slip him some money. The kid handed him the other note. "Thanks."

Everis closed and locked the door. "The Silencer started killing before coming to Highland Springs." He set the box on the coffee table and lifted the lid. The aroma of baked cheese filled the room.

Shar's stomach growled. "Maybe he's always lived here and never hunted in his own backyard before." She perched on the edge of the sofa and snatched a slice of pizza. "What does the other note say?"

"It's just a name. Maggie Olsen."

"It doesn't sound familiar." She dialed Mayfield's number. "See what you can find out on a Maggie Olsen."

"Pretty common name. Is Maggie short for something?"

"That's all I've got, Mark. Thanks." She hung up and tossed the crust of her pizza to Goliath who caught it midair. She smiled. Why had she waited so long to get a dog?

The front door opened, and Shar and Everis both drew their weapons. Candy stepped into the room. "Whoa. I surrender." She eyed Goliath, then the pizza. "Yum." She dropped her purse and grabbed a piece, flopping down next to Shar. "Why are y'all so jumpy?"

"We've had a visitor leaving notes." Everis threw the bolt on the front door. "Don't leave this unlocked."

"Is that why we have the horse?" She nodded toward Goliath.

"Mr. Berkemeyer gave him to me. He's moving away and selling the junkyard. The dog's name is

Goliath."

"He's massive." Candy rubbed the dog's head. "But absolutely adorable."

"Do you know a Maggie?" Shar reached for another slice of pizza.

Candy thought for a moment. "I know a Margaret Olsen. Don't you remember her? She taught study hall when we were in high school. Oh, wait. She quit before you had her class."

"What do you know about her?" Shar glanced to where Everis stood at the window, peering outside.

"Old." Candy laughed. "Of course, she could have been thirty, and we would have thought her old at the time. Pretty, a little plump. I don't know if she was married or had kids. Why all the questions?"

Using her toe, Shar pushed the paper with the woman's name across the coffee table. "Left on the porch."

"Hmm. There's a Maggie that lives up the mountain, but I don't think her last name is Olsen."

"She could have married." Shar's to-do list continued to grow. They still hadn't contacted any of the women with question marks next to their names, and now they added a mystery woman to the list.

"I hope you have an extra pillow," Everis said, "because I'm sleeping here tonight."

"Why?" Shar narrowed her eyes. "Did you not hear me when I said I wasn't helpless?"

"I heard you." He marched to the kitchen, then up the stairs.

"What's he doing?" Candy craned her neck.

"Checking the doors and windows is my guess." Shar sighed and stood. "I'm too tired to argue with him, so I'll get a blanket from the closet."

"Should I be scared?"

"Not with Everis and Goliath here. The three of us will protect you." Shar bopped her sister on the head. "You've never been worried before with just me."

"I've never had a killer come this close to the house before." Candy closed the pizza box and carried it and it's few slices to the kitchen. "Where's the dog going to sleep?"

"Wherever he wants." Shar chuckled and motioned for Goliath to follow. She'd gone a few steps when the doorbell rang. She leaned against the wood. "Who is it?"

"Pet delivery."

"Leave it. Thank you." When she heard the sound of a car driving away, Shar opened the door, dragged in the fifty-pound bag, then relocked the door. Everis had one night to play the hero. She wasn't going to be a prisoner in her home. She had a killer to catch and a town to make safe again.

* * *

The Silencer headed through the trees back to his car. He was getting tired of the game. Tired of his job. Except for him, nothing happened in Highland Springs. Now that he was on the prowl, folks were more cautious. Maybe it was time to reveal his identity and raise the stakes.

How would his darling sisters react when they found out who he was? He laughed, the sound ringing through the trees. He glanced behind him. He was far enough away they couldn't hear in the house.

He'd been so close to snatching the pretty new receptionist. Now, she'd be on her guard and Sharlene and the agent more vigilant than ever. They were getting close. Rather than lose the upper hand, The Silencer needed a plan that would keep him on top. He wouldn't be caught until he was ready, then he'd go out in a blaze of glory and take his sisters with him.

He stowed the bow in the trunk of his car and drove home to chat with a lovely lady by the name of Ann.

Everis lay on the sofa, staring through the dark at the ceiling for hours. Occasionally, Goliath came out to check on him. A branch, blown by the wind, scraped against the window. It wasn't those things that kept him awake. It was the fact that Shar slept a few doors down the hall.

What an idiot. They were chasing the most dangerous man he'd had the misfortune to hear of, and all he could do was think of how good Shar's legs had looked in those shorts. He flung his arm over his eyes and groaned before sliding his legs off the too-short sofa and standing.

He might as well put the coffee on and start breakfast. They had a full day ahead of them.

While he filled the reservoir to the Keurig, he glanced out the window over the sink. A shadow moved in the trees catching his attention. Everis stared harder. He hit the floor a breath before a bullet shattered the glass.

"Everis." Shar, gun in hand, called from the doorway, a pair of slip-on canvas shoes on her feet. "Do you have the shooter in sight?"

"I did." He pulled himself up and peered through the window. "This is not like The Silencer."

"No, it isn't." Shar stood and barged out the kitchen

door before Everis could stop her.

"Come out of there right now or I will shoot you!" She stormed toward the trees, Everis on her heels.

An elderly man, hands held high, rifle slung across his shoulders, stepped out. "I didn't mean to shoot at your house."

"Wilmer Hopkins, I'm throwing your drunk ass in jail." She wiggled her fingers at Everis.

"What? My handcuffs are in the house."

She growled. "Hand me your rifle, Wilmer, then start walking toward the house."

"It was an accident."

"I can smell the whiskey on your breath from here. Hunting and liquor don't mix. Let's add in the fact it isn't hunting season." She handed the rifle to Everis and gave the old man a shove.

Everis stayed behind them. He vowed right then and there that he didn't ever want to be on the receiving end of an angry Shar. He'd seen her mad, but this was enraged. Frightening and mesmerizing at the same time.

"What is that?" Wilmer froze in the doorway to the kitchen.

"That is the dog that's going to guard you. Sit down." She shoved Wilmer into a chair. "Goliath, watch him. I'm going to go change. Everis, I'll meet you at the station."

"Are you sure? I can take Mr. Hopkins with me."

"No need for formalities," Wilmer said. "Besides, I'm not going anywhere soon, it appears. I think this dog is drooling."

Everis grinned. "I'd be more afraid of the sheriff than the dog." He called out to Shar that he'd meet her after he went home and changed.

By the time Everis arrived at the station, Mr. Hopkins was snoring in the holding cell and a very large woman was screaming at a stony-faced Shar to release her husband. Just another day in Highland Springs. He was quickly starting to love it there.

Shar kept one hand on Goliath's head. The dog looked as if it wanted to take a meaty bite out of the woman, but to his credit, he kept his dark eyes trained on her and remained still.

"Mrs. Hopkins, your husband shot out my kitchen window where Agent Hayes was fixing coffee. He could very well have killed the agent." Shar's eyes flashed.

"A man spent the night?" Mrs. Hopkins clutched the collar of her—was that a muumuu? "Shameful."

"Ma'am, I slept on the couch as protection for the fine Camenetti women. Would you be more comfortable in the conference room? We've a nice sofa in there you can wait on." Everis took the woman by the elbow and steered her into the conference. "Can I get you anything? Water, soda, or coffee?"

"Coffee. Lots of cream." The woman waddled to the vinyl sofa at one end of the room. "Convince the sheriff to release my husband."

"I'll see what I can do." Everis kept his smile in place until the door closed behind him. Release her husband? Not likely. He wanted to throttle the old fool.

"How do you do that?" Shar crossed her arms.

"Do what?" He tilted his head.

"Calm the beasts with a simple smile."

"Because he's pretty," Natalie said, handing Shar a stack of messages. "Oh, and Mark said he's found some information on the name you gave him. He'll be late, then he'll fill you in."

"I'm not pretty." Everis shook his head. "The word you're looking for is handsome or manly."

Natalie scrunched up her nose. "Delusional."

Shar visibly relaxed and glanced toward the conference room. "What do we do with Mrs. Hopkins?"

Everis clapped her on the shoulder. "No idea. You're the sheriff." Whistling, he headed to her office.

"Thanks a lot," she called after him.

In Shar's office, he pulled up the dummy social media account and read through the messages. He was ready to click out when a message came through.

I was very disappointed that my evening with the pretty Natalie was ruined by the authorities. Obviously, she is working with you to trap me. Yes, I'm The Silencer, and you're on my list, Sheriff Camenetti.

Chapter Fifteen

"Well, darn." Shar plopped into her office chair and stared at the message on her screen. "Maybe this means he'll stop killing and focus solely on me." She tried to keep a brave face, but in reality her insides had turned to frozen sludge.

She'd faced into the barrel of a gun before, fought with a hyped-up druggie and come out the victor, but this was the first time an alleged blood relative wanted to kill her. It messed with a person's head.

"I'm moving in with you and Candy until this guy is caught." The determined expression on Everis's face sent a clear message that he wouldn't argue the fact.

"Suit yourself." Shar shut off her laptop. "Let's start knocking on doors and collecting DNA starting with Mark, Ben, Lars, and the cameraman. One of them is the killer." She hoped. Otherwise, they were back at square one.

"Let me make a phone call." Everis pressed buttons on his phone. "Agent Hayes here. Tell me you have something for me." Everis nodded several times, then hung up. "Your father is definitely related to our perp. Let's get the rest of the DNA from our suspects." He stood. "We're getting close, sweetheart."

"I still held out a sliver of hope that the killer wasn't a relative, much less a brother. Half-brother.

Whatever." She marched ahead of him and passed the reception desk. "Save any cup from any male who gets a drink of water from the cooler," she told Natalie. "Cigarettes, gum—anything we can collect DNA on. Get Mark Arnes, Ben Wilson, Lars Townsend, and Luke Ball in here to take a DNA test. If they refuse, get a warrant."

Shock waves rolled through her the realization that her father had spawned a killer. She wanted to curl up under the blankets in her room and not come out until the nightmare had ended. Being sheriff of a small town in the Ozarks should have been a simple job of keeping the peace...not hunting a serial killer.

She reached for the front door, stepping back when Everis moved in front of her. "I take the lead from now on," he told her.

"A bullet can take you down as easily as me."

He cut her a glance. "Yes, but then when I'm down, you'll take down the perp. This town needs you. I'm only on loan."

A lump formed in her throat at the reminder he would leave once the case closed. It shouldn't matter. She'd pledged herself to her career a long time ago. Still, she couldn't help but wonder what if he stayed?

Shar whirled back to the reception desk. "I'm sending you and my sister to a mountain cabin. I'm assuming you're capable of protecting her?"

Natalie nodded. "I am a federal agent."

"Good. Everis, come with me to the shop. Natalie, please let me know once you have contacted the men for DNA." She shoved open the door, despite Everis's protests, and hurried to her jeep.

"I said to let me go first," Everis said, sliding into

the passenger side.

"You aren't my protector. We're partners in this." She turned the key in the ignition and roared form the parking lot toward the salon where her sister worked.

"Does anyone know about this cabin?"

"Just my…" she called her father via blue tooth. "Does anyone know about our mountain cabin?"

"Who is this?"

"It's Sharlene. This is important." She shot a frustrated glance at Everis.

"Are you in danger?"

"Dad!" The word burst out of her before she could stop it.

"Nobody knows. Just you and Candice. You're scaring me, sweetheart."

"I'm sending Candice there."

"I'll go, too. I can keep her safe."

Shar glanced at Everis who nodded. "Alright. I'll pick you up in thirty minutes. Don't tell anyone unless you want Candy dead." She pressed the button on her steering wheel, disconnecting the call. "The more the merrier, right?"

"It's best. We have no proof that the man your father sired won't come after him in an act of vengeance."

She hadn't thought of that. Anything her mysterious half-brother had against her, he would also have against his other family members. Time was running out. "We don't know who this man's mother is. She could also be in danger."

"Let's get your sister and father settled, then we'll hold another press conference. You'll have to air some dirty laundry in order to warn a woman we don't know."

She'd parade through town in her underwear if it would stop one more person from dying. Pulling up to the salon door, she rushed inside. "Candy, you're finished for the day. Let's go."

Her sister scowled from where she washed a customer's hair. She opened her lips to protest, then nodded and asked another stylist to take over. "Let me get my purse." She disappeared into a backroom, returning seconds later. She didn't speak again until they were in the jeep. "Explain, please."

Everis turned sideways in the seat. "We're sending you and your father into the mountains. Agent Larson will accompany you. You have time to pack a bag of necessities before you leave by nightfall."

Shar glanced through the rearview mirror at her sister's pale face. "There's no doubt that The Silencer is related to us. A half-brother. He's outright said he's coming after me, which could also mean you."

"Can I take the dog?" She glanced at her lap. "Never mind. You'll need that monster more than me."

"I'll be staying in your house until this is over, Candy. I'll take care of Shar." Everis reached across and laid his hand on hers. "I promise."

Candy took a deep shuddering breath. "Okay. I'll tell work I had an emergency. I can look at the bright side of this."

"Which is?" Shar glanced in the mirror again.

"I'll get to know our father."

Unfortunately, so would Shar, something she hadn't planned on ever doing. She parked in front of her father's house and honked the horn.

He dashed out, a suitcase in hand, and climbed into

the backseat with Candy. "Let's get the hell out of here."

*

"We're picking up Agent Larson. She'll accompany you." Everis glanced at the gun on the man's hip. He started to ask whether he had a permit, then shrugged. A weapon would come in handy, permit or not. He just prayed the man knew how to use one.

Natalie was waiting for them when they arrived. "All the men on the list except for Lars will be in this afternoon. What are you going to do about a receptionist?"

"Call a temp agency, I guess." Shar handed her a slip of paper. "Call as soon as you arrive. It won't take more than two hours. The place was fully stocked when I left two months ago."

She nodded, grabbing a large black bag from under her desk. "Ready, Mr. and Miss Camenetti? It won't pay to dawdle. I'm parked out back, so we can leave without being observed."

Shar hugged her sister. "Please, stay safe. You, too." She stared stony-faced at her father.

"We will." He patted her shoulder. "See you soon. I'm really sorry my past has come back to haunt us this way." He pivoted and marched out the back door.

"We'll be okay. It's you I'm worried about." Candy hugged Shar again, then whirled to face Everis. "If anything happens to her, I'll come after you." She followed Natalie out the door.

The front door opened seconds after and Mark, Ben, and Luke waltzed in, laughing about being suspects. Idiots. "This way, gentlemen." Everis motioned them into the conference room. "This is fast and painless.

Where's Townsend?"

Luke shrugged. "Didn't show up for work this morning."

Everis met Shar's shocked look, then asked, "Did anyone try to call him? Go by his place?"

"He's a grown man. He doesn't need a babysitter."

"Mark." Shar called into the hallway. "Go by Townsend's house. Get me some DNA."

"Yes, boss." He threw her a salute and rushed away.

Everis had a feeling in the pit of his stomach. By this time tomorrow, they'd know the identity of The Silencer. He swabbed the mouths of each of the men and dropped the swab into individual bags. He was also fairly certain it wouldn't be one of these three.

"Thank you, gentlemen. That's all we need."

While he took the DNA samples, Shar was on the phone arranging a press conference.

"Reporters will be here within the hour. We'll run live." She marched to her office.

Once Everis arranged for a courier, he joined her. "Are you okay?"

"Let me think." She leaned back in her chair and crossed her arms. "My family is in danger and exiled from their homes. I need a bodyguard. My half-brother, who I strongly suspect may be Lars Townsend, is a serial killer bent on some twisted form of revenge. All because my father couldn't keep his pants zipped forty years ago. Does that answer your question?"

"I'm sorry." He perched on the corner of her desk and cupped her cheek. "I wish I could make it all go away."

She clenched her teeth and nodded, then ducked her head. "Maybe I'm not cut out for this job. Shouldn't I have known Lars was a killer?"

"I didn't, and I'm excellent at my job." Of course, he'd been chasing this man for more than a year, but he was quite good at hiding his tracks. "What I'd like to know is why he's now coming forward? Why not confront you when he started killing?"

"Something triggered him."

"The death of his mother perhaps?" Everis brushed Shar's hair back, then straightened. "Maybe he just recently found out who his father is. It's quite possible he's a sociopath who just found out who the rest of his family is."

"That has to be it." She grabbed her cell. "Mark. Are you there? Any sign of Lars? Get me a hairbrush, anything. Also, look for personal papers that may have the name of his mother. Call me as soon as you have something."

The phone on her desk rang. Shar answered. "We'll be right there." She hung up. "Loud voices next door to Mrs. Latham's house. I really need to get a receptionist quick or I'll be answering calls all day." She pressed a button on her desk phone and stood.

"You don't seem too worried."

"The couple next to Mrs. Latham are as old as Methuselah and drink as much as a fish. They're always fighting. I'm out there at least once a week."

"They aren't a danger to each other?"

"No, but Mrs. Latham is a danger to them." They headed for her jeep. "Last time, she set a bag of dog poop on fire and threw it at their front door. Nothing I say to any of them does any good."

He grinned. "They're a decent distraction when you're waiting for evidence."

She laughed. "That they are."

Lars wanted to shoot Mayfield in the head. Instead, watched the man pilfer through his belongings. It was a good thing. Shar knowing exactly who he was fit in with his plan. The cancer that ate at his prostrate would take him within a matter of months. He didn't intend to die that way. He'd do so on his own terms with his darling sisters and philandering father joining him.

He ducked and made his way around the corner of the house. Whistling, he straightened and strolled toward his car a few doors down. He had another place to stay. This house was his mother's house, once upon a time. How long until they found her buried in the backyard? When she'd informed him of his real father's identity, he'd lost it. But when she told him she knew he was the Little Rock killer, that put him over the edge. He'd picked up the closest thing at hand and smashed it over her head. The antique iron had done the trick.

If he could wipe all his siblings off the face of the planet, he would, but he'd come across several dead-ends while searching. His mother hadn't known the identity of the other women in Camenetti's life. Lars had to be content with ridding the world of his father and sisters.

Chapter Sixteen

"Lars Townsend's mother is Maggie Olsen." Mark dropped a newspaper article encased in a plastic sleeve on Shar's desk. "She disappeared ten years ago. He lives in her house." He sat in the chair opposite her. "It wasn't hard to find the information. The man keeps impeccable records. This was on his desk in plain sight. He wanted us to find it."

Shar glanced to where the name Maggie Olsen was circled in red. Off to the side with an arrow pointing at the name was one word. Mother. "Hire someone to dig up the yard. My guess is Lars killed his mother."

But why? So many questions still left unanswered. Why was the man driven to erase his family *and* strangers rather than one or the other? Could it simply be that he had a hunger for blood, and a swift finish to his family wasn't part of his plan? Most serial killers left their family alone. Not her brother.

"We really need another deputy or two." Shar scooted the article back across her desk. "Put this in evidence. I doubt there's much need for fingerprint check. We know who The Silencer is."

"Crazy that he's your brother. Wow." Mayfield stood. "Didn't see that coming."

"Yeah, real crazy. Where's Agent Hayes?"

"Greeting the temporary receptionist. I never thought I'd say this, but I miss Amber. This new lady is a real grouch." He took the newspaper and left Shar to her thoughts.

Not a place she wanted to be. She checked emails, and her day brightened to find out they were getting another full-time deputy arriving tomorrow. That would allow Shar the freedom to focus solely on taking down Lars and leave the daily disturbances to Mayfield and the new guy.

Feeling years older than her thirty-five, she pushed to her feet and moved to the front hall. She stopped short at the sight of Everis failing in his attempt to charm the grossly overweight woman behind the desk. The chair protested when she swiveled to face Shar.

"Sheriff, I must confess there are certain things lacking."

"Ma'am?"

"I need a sturdier chair. This one squeaks. Not to mention there's no fridge under the desk. I'm not capable of moving around. That's why I take reception-type jobs. I also don't like dogs."

"Sheriff Camenetti, meet Alice Jones." Everis rolled his eyes.

Shar put on her mask and squared her shoulders, then motioned for Goliath to sit beside her. "We will get you a bigger chair." She ignored the narrowing of the woman's eyes. "We have a refrigerator in the lounge. I don't think it professional for a receptionist to eat at her desk. The restroom is down the hall, unless you also demand a porta-potty. If these conditions are not up to your standards, feel free to leave. Now, if you don't mind, Ms. Jones, we have more pressing business to attend to." Shar marched out the front door.

Everis hurried after her. "You really don't care if you get shot, do you?"

She shrugged one shoulder. "You, me, Mayfield...we're all at risk."

"Where are we going?"

"My dear brother's house."

Within fifteen minutes, she parked in front of a two-story house she'd passed almost every day of her life. Now, she remembered Miss Olsen. A pretty, bitter woman who bore a child out of wedlock and took out her disappointment on her students. Having called the woman *Old Sour Face* for so many years, Shar had forgotten her real name.

Her father had a lot more to answer for than siring a crazy son. He'd ruined a lot of lives in his whoring days.

"You okay?" Everis's warm gaze gave her the strength to open the vehicle door.

"Yep." She was the sheriff. She couldn't dwell on what-ifs until a killer was caught. Then, it was quite possible she'd require psychiatric help.

"Are we looking for anything in particular?"

"A place to bury a body." Shar headed to the backyard by way of a cute white picket fence. Goliath ran ahead, quickly marking his territory.

Close to half an acre of yard, surrounded by oak trees and a massive magnolia tree, would make digging take longer than Shar wanted. Unless...she moved to the magnolia tree directly in the center of the yard. "How old do you think this is?"

He grinned. "I'd say it's about ten-years-old."

"Yep." If not for the mention of Miss Olsen being

from Magnolia, Arkansas, she wouldn't have thought a thing of the beautiful tree. Now, she knew without a doubt they'd find the woman's body buried under it. "It'll be a shame to chop this down."

Goliath disappeared into a shed at the far end of the property. When he didn't return at Shar's whistle, she strode in that direction.

"Here, boy." She ducked into the dark room. "Everis, you might want to see this."

A plank of wood lay on top of two aluminum sawhorses. On top of the plank were the skeletal remains of a body. Strips of fabric hung from the wrists and ankles. From the purse and shoes next to the makeshift table, the body was that of a woman.

Everis ducked in and gave a low whistle. "I think this might be Susan Moray, his first victim. She disappeared over a year ago and set me on this cross-state chase." He pulled a pair of gloves from his pocket and snapped them on his hands before opening the purse. "Yes, it's her."

Shar walked around the table. "She'd been tortured. Was he filming back then?"

"Not that we know of."

"At least the family will have closure. Were all the others recovered?" She studied the array of tools on a low shelf. Suspicious stains marred the surface.

"Yes. This is the only one he took away."

"A trophy."

Guilt over the amount of women Townsend had killed after Moray rushed through Everis's mind. His head told him he had no way of knowing the killer lived in the small Ozark community of Highland Springs, or that he had brought Moray here to kill her. His heart told him he'd failed multiple times.

If any man other than a reporter had shown up at every crime scene, he would have immediately grown suspicious. It wasn't a mistake he would make again.

"I'll call to have the place taped off and investigated." Shar left, Goliath trotting at her heels.

Everis continued to study the shed and its array of tools designed to cause pain and death. Why Moray? Why was she the first? His thoughts took him back to her purse. One by one, he pulled out the items inside. A mirror, lady's personal things, a lipstick, a wallet, a pink can of pepper spray. It didn't look as if it had ever been used. She'd either known Townsend or agreed to meet him for the first time. Either way, she didn't feel threatened.

He pulled out her driver's license. Behind it was an identification card for Susan Moray, Oncologist. He put everything back in the purse and went to find Shar.

He found her stringing yellow crime-scene tape across the front yard. "We need Townsend's medical records."

"That shouldn't be too hard to get. Why?"

"Susan Moray was an oncologist."

"His or his mother's?"

"That's what we need to find out." Everis turned as the medical examiner arrived. "The body is in the shed in back."

The man nodded and headed that way, accompanied by two medics with a gurney. Everis pushed open the front door. The house still looked as if a woman from the seventies lived there. Heavy furniture with cushions depicting animals and forests in a hideous orange. A green shag carpet—enough said. The kitchen had Formica countertops and white-washed cabinets. Someone had tried to update a bit.

He continued down the hallway and glanced into the only modern room in the house. Townsend's office. Mayfield had done a good job of searching while leaving things orderly. Some officers were in too big of a hurry and left things a mess. Past the office were a bathroom and two bedrooms. One done in floral fabrics, the other in dark blues and greens. He chose to enter Townsend's room.

A closet with glass doors rimmed in gold brass took up one whole wall. Everis slid the door open. A hiss was the last thing he heard.

* * *

Shar's phone rang. "Sheriff Camenetti."

"Hello, dear sis."

"Lars." Her voice could have put out a fire with its iciness.

"I have cameras all around my mother's property. Would you like to know what I just saw?"

"Stop playing games. You won't win this."

"Unfortunately, I won't. The cancer will get me, but not before I take the rest of you down with me. Why not spend eternity with the family I was denied?"

"You're crazy."

"Tsk tsk. Do you want to know about Agent Hayes or not?"

"What about him?" Her heart slowed.

"There isn't much time for you to give him the antidote. He's been gassed by Tabun, sis. Hurry. The antidote is in the nightstand. This is only a warning for him to go away." Click.

Shar raced into the house, glancing in each room until she spotted Everis on the floor of a bedroom. She yanked open drawers, finally pulling out a syringe. "Please be the antidote and not more poison." She yanked off the top, tapped the cylinder, and plunged it into Everis's arm. Immediately after, she dialed 911.

"He's breathing, but unresponsive. May have been given Tabun. I've administered what I think is the antidote. What else do I need to do?" She put her phone on speaker and set it on the carpet next to her.

"Get him out of that room and outside to fresh air. Sheriff, you've been exposed to a much smaller dose, but time is imperative."

Shar shoved the phone into her pocket and grabbed Everis by the legs. She dragged him down the hall until she reached the front door, then struggled to get his arm around her shoulders. Once she had, she struggled to her feet and stumbled outside, tumbling both of them down the stairs.

She lay in the dirt, taking huge gulps of air and stared into the branches of a crepe myrtle. Staring down at her was the blinking red eye of a camera. She flipped the camera the bird, then closed her eyes.

When she woke, she was in the back of an ambulance, oxygen mask on her face. She removed the mask. "Agent Hayes?"

"In the other ambulance. Your quick thinking saved his life." The paramedic squeezed her shoulder. "Mask on. Just relax."

Shar's eyes drifted closed. Her last thought was how badly she wanted to shoot Lars.

Chapter Seventeen

Forty-eight hours later and recently discharged from the hospital, Shar returned to her house with Everis. She'd had Mayfield and the new deputy, who she had yet to meet, carefully find and remove all cameras from Lars's home. They'd found several in each room, the shed, and outside. He'd watched their every move, releasing the gas via remote when Everis opened the closet. Her crazy brother was smart. Maybe too smart.

"Is it too much to ask that he die before anyone else?" She unlocked her front door, pleased to see Mayfield had taken care of Goliath. The dog almost folded himself in wagging his tail so hard upon seeing her. Shar wrapped her arms around his neck. "Good boy. I missed you."

"I'm the one who almost died." Everis grinned. "Can I have a hug?"

She stepped into his arms. "I'm glad you didn't die." She gazed into his dark eyes. "You really scared me." Resting her cheek against his chest, she listened to his heart. Just for a moment she wanted to succumb to simply being a woman and not the sheriff. For a few seconds, she wanted to relish in the feel of his strong arms around her.

A sharp rap on the door jolted them apart as if they

were teenagers caught doing something naughty. Shar smiled up at Everis and peered through the peephole. Mayfield and a middle-aged man, most likely the new deputy, waited. "Everis, I need to look more professional before meeting the new guy. Will you let them in?" She thundered up the stairs. Meeting the newest addition to the sheriff's department in ragged jeans would not make a good impression.

Dressed in a clean uniform, hair tied back into a ponytail, Shar headed back downstairs. All three men stood when she entered the living room. She held out her hand to the new deputy. "I'm Sheriff Camenetti. I am so glad you're here."

He didn't look happy to see her. "Deputy Ted Pinson, formerly of St. Louis, Missouri."

Hmm. She'd bet her hat he wasn't happy about working for a woman. The man stood at five-foot-nine, handsome, a head of dark hair greying at the temples, and a big macho attitude. Candy would swoon when she saw him. "I think you'll love Highland Springs. I trust you've studied the case board?"

He nodded.

"Any ideas we may not have thought of?" Shar tried meeting the deputy's gaze, but he looked everywhere but at her.

He glanced at Everis. "There's been no more filming of deaths, which I assume means he's lying low."

"Speak to the sheriff, deputy." Everis sat on the sofa and crossed his ankles on the coffee table. "I'm only here to help."

The deputy's face darkened. He glanced at Shar, then turned on his heel and marched outside.

"He's quite pleasant, isn't he?" Shar seized her gun belt. "Let's go catch a killer, boys." And, hopefully, put a certain deputy in his place by proving she was up to the job she was voted into.

Mayfield greeted them on the steps of the station. "Sorry about Pinson." He shrugged. "He was sent here as punishment for a bad attitude against women in law enforcement."

"Lucky me." Shar frowned. As if she didn't have enough weighing her down. Now, she had to prove herself to a man who had his mind made up that she wasn't cut out for the job. Everis needed to hurry up with her super-sized coffee. The sludge in the lounge wasn't on her agenda this morning. "Let's meet in the conference room in fifteen minutes."

She stopped by the reception desk to collect her messages—heaven forbid the woman should bring them to her—and forced a smile and a good morning. Shar hurried away, purportedly glancing through the pink slips of paper. But the receptionist's loud harangue reached her office—dogs didn't belong in a place of. Shar ignored her and read the messages. They really needed to get more modern.

One complaint of hoodlums ripping up saplings. Another of parties late in the night by the lake. Typical small-town crime. Thank goodness no more dead bodies. Not seeing anything that required immediate attention, she set the papers on her desk and headed for the conference room.

Mayfield had printed out an 8 x 10 glossy of Lars's driver's license. Shar picked it up off the table and tacked it to the case board. They had the identity of their killer, now they needed to apprehend him. Easier said than done.

"Coffee." Everis came up behind her and handed her a large cup. "What are you thinking?"

"That we need to set a trap."

"Nope." He took a sip of his drink. "He'll come without us deliberately putting you out there. We tried with Natalie, and it didn't work. He won't be easily tricked."

"Lars won't do anything unless he thinks he can get my entire family at the same time."

"You'd risk them?"

She shot him a look. "No. But we can let him think they'll be with me. Think about it. The idea has merit."

She stiffened as Mayfield and Pinson entered the room, the dog-eying her. "If you have a problem with me, Deputy, I can make sure you're transferred elsewhere."

"No problem." He took a seat, a muscle ticking in his jaw.

"Good. Now wipe the sullen look off your face and help us catch this guy." Shar sat at the head of the table. "I'm trying to convince Agent Hayes to use me as bait."

All three men's gazes locked on hers.

* * *

Lars paced the small hotel room. Inactivity drove him insane. He had a young woman who had agreed to meet with him that evening, but his excitement dimmed. Mere days separated him from taking his family with him. Pain from the cancer had started filling his body, interfering with his sleep. He didn't have much time left.

Through dusty sheers that poked between the gold-fabric curtains, he stared out at the parking lot. Where were the old man and Candy? Worse-case scenario, he'd take Shar down with him, but he really wanted all three. He would spend eternity with the family he'd been denied, wherever that was.

Oh, he wasn't a fool to think there weren't more siblings, there were. He didn't know who they were, but one, and he was seeing her tomorrow. The not knowing the identity of the others ate at him as badly as the cancer.

Killing dulled the ache. With each scream of his victims, his pain ebbed. Killing had medicinal purposes. He smiled. Maybe he would go through with his date that evening after all. He needed to find a way to catch the pretty thing by surprise. He'd seen his face plastered across the television with last night's news.

He watched the young maid exit a room across the way. She was an easy target. Ten years ago, he would have taken her. But now that he knew his father met his mother through a classified ad in the paper, he had to find his victims in a similar way. It just made things a bit more complicated.

* * *

"I told you no, Shar." Everis plunked his cup hard enough on the table that coffee shot up out of the sipping hole.

She slapped her hands flat on the table and stood. "I'm the sheriff. What I say goes."

"There it is." Pinson smirked.

If looks could kill, Shar's gaze would have riddled him with holes. "We will discuss your animosity toward all things female when Lars Townsend is behind bars. Until then, you keep your mouth shut unless you're contributing something useful. Got it?"

"Got it, boss lady." Pinson leaned back in his chair.

Mayfield twirled a pencil. "I'm all for the sheriff stepping out there if it gets rid of Attila the Hun out front."

Shar grinned and sat back down. "Not the support I was looking for, but I'll take what I can get. Let's make a plan, gentlemen, because we are setting a trap, whether you agree with me or not." She locked gazes with Everis. Her mask had slipped into place, shutting him out. "I will confront Lars on television later this afternoon, challenging him to come forward. I'm sure he's watching the news, which is why he's gone into hiding."

Everis shook his head and stared at the tabletop. This plan of hers could end very badly for more people than just her. When she'd finished speaking her mind, telling the others how things were going to be, he stood and stormed from the conference room. Needing a place to cool down, and not able to use an office that wasn't his, he entered the men's room and locked the door.

With hands planted on the sink, he stared into the drain. Her plan would probably work. What kept him from agreeing with her was fear. Black, undulating, suffocating fear.

The murders Lars had done and filmed were bad enough. If he got his hands on Shar and filmed her death and torture, everyone in Highland Springs would be affected, and his heart would stop beating.

Somehow, he needed to rein in his emotions. He didn't desire a long-term relationship and wouldn't dare ask Shar to step down from a job she loved. No, his heart would have to get used to the fact that love, marriage, and all that went with it was out of the question for him and Shar. It would be safer for him to steer clear of all romantic entanglements.

He lifted his head and looked in the mirror. The face of a haunted man stared back. He took a deep breath, then let it out slowly. Again, then again, until he felt ready to face the others.

Let Shar come up with her plan. Everis would make plans of his own.

"Ready to agree?" Shar glanced up from her desk when he entered.

"Resigned." He sat across from her. "What time is the press conference?"

"Five o'clock. We'll be live on KARK." She tilted her head. "This has to be done, Everis. Lars needs to be brought to justice before more women die."

"Now that is something I can agree on." He placed his right ankle on his left knee. "We'll go along with whatever you cook up, but you can count on me being glued to your side every minute of every day, twenty-four seven. I hope you're ready for a roommate, sweetheart, because we're sharing a room."

She narrowed her eyes. "We are not."

"We are. No hanky-panky." He chuckled wryly. "But where you go, I go. When you're in the bathroom, I'm leaning against the door with one ear plastered to the wood."

"We'll talk about this later." With those words, she dismissed him and turned to her laptop.

At five o'clock on the dot, Shar stood behind a podium placed on the top step of the sheriff's office and faced the reporters. She stiffened when Everis stepped forward, standing one foot back and to her right. He stifled a grin. Let her stew. He'd been serious about staying close. He scanned the onlookers, searching for Townsend.

Shar held up her hand to still the crowd. "This is directed toward The Silencer, aka Lars Townsend." She leaned forward. "You're a coward that preys on women. If you have a grievance against me and mine, then step forward and face me." A cold smile spread her lips. "Or perhaps, my dear brother, you're afraid of me. If not, you should be. I will release the hounds of hell on your heels and use everything in my disposal to make sure you pay for your crimes. Good day." She spun around and entered the building.

Everis approached the podium. "No questions." He joined Shar inside and, without speaking, followed her to her office.

Chapter Eighteen

Shar banged pans onto the stove as she prepared that evening's meal. Why she felt compelled to cook for the thorn in her side she had no idea.

She broke spaghetti noodles into the boiling water, spilling some onto the floor where Goliath made short work of them. Behind her was the soft chomp chomp of the knife Everis used to cut vegetables for their salad.

"Be as angry as you want, Shar," Everis said, "but I won't be changing my mind."

"I'm not talking to you." She took a bread knife and sliced down the French loaf. When she'd hacked away at what would become garlic toast, she mixed garlic powder and softened butter into a paste.

"You're being childish."

She whirled, a knife clutched in her hand. "You're being a chauvinistic boar!"

He stood and set down his larger knife. "Put the knife down, darlin'. I'm coming closer."

"Why?" She backed against the counter holding the knife like a sword.

"I'm going to show you why I'm acting so heavy-handed with you." He stepped forward.

"Keep your distance."

"Prepare yourself, sweetheart, because I'm going to kiss some sense into you."

She thrust the knife forward.

Everis dodged the weapon and gripped her wrist. Eyes smoldering and locked on hers, he removed the knife and dropped it into the sink. He lifted her as if she weighed nothing and plopped her on the counter, so her face was even with his. "Ready?"

Her heart lodged in her throat. "We shouldn't do this, Everis. Someday one of us is walking out that door, leaving the other behind."

"Shut up." He ran his hands up her bare legs and stepped between them. "There's no harm in kissing. No damage done with shoving aside the evil in this world, if even for a few minutes." He cupped her face in his hands. "Ready?"

"No," she whispered. Her traitorous body shifted forward. Her hands clutched his shoulders.

A smile teased at his lips as he pressed them to hers. Softly, his tongue teasing, before the kiss deepened, and he held her as close as was physically possible. She moaned deep in her throat for more. Starved for him, she wrapped her legs around his waist. Her heart raced, making it hard to breathe—so lost was she in his embrace.

The water boiled over, hissing on the burner. She reached to turn it off. Her fingers connected with the burner, causing a small gasp, an intake of air.

Everis pulled back, quickly assessing the situation. He turned her hand over. Blisters formed on her fingertips. He scooped up the butter mixture and spread it across them. A smile formed on his lips.

"What is so funny? I'm injured." She tried to pull her hand away, her breathing irregular. Whether from pain or passion, she wasn't sure.

"I was thinking of how we were saved by fire." He peered up at her from under lowered lashes. "Things were really starting to heat up, no pun intended."

"Seriously, you can be such an idiot." She jumped to the floor, fighting back her own grin. "Thank you for the distraction."

"I'm always willing." He moved back to the salad, leaving her warmed and feeling safe.

It wouldn't last, but she would embrace the feeling for now.

She soon had spaghetti and bread on the table. Everis brought the salad. Instead of sitting across from her, he chose the seat beside her. He poured them each a glass of wine. "Smells good."

"I make a killer sauce." She liked sitting at the table with someone for supper. She and Candy usually ate in front of the television. "I wish it was safe to call Candy."

"Not worth the call getting traced." He filled his plate with noodles and sauce.

"No salad?"

"Rabbit food." His eyes twinkled. "This is nice. Not as good as the kiss, but definitely worthy of eating."

She laughed, her face heating. "We shouldn't do that. You'll be leaving soon."

His smile faded. "Yes, I will. The reason I don't want you putting yourself as bait is because I can't live in this world without you in it." He raised a hand to stop her when she started to speak. "I know there can't be anything serious between us. I live in Little Rock and you here. We're both married to our jobs. But, even after I leave, I'll know you still walk these streets, Shar."

What could she say to that? Tears filled her eyes. "I can't back down."

"You don't always have to prove yourself."

"I do. The world is full of men like Pinson. Too many who believe I'm not cut out for this job. There is already talk of not voting me back in the next election. People are scared and want the killing to stop. I'd rather face Lars on my terms, not his."

He reached over and took her hand. "We'll face him, Shar. Not you. We."

"And then you'll leave." The words almost lodged in her throat.

A shadow crossed his features. "And then I'll leave."

Lars waited in the bushes next to the sign at a seedy motel on the outskirts of town. Sally, what a quaint old name, couldn't be as sweet as she made herself out to be. She didn't balk at meeting him in such a place. He already had the room set up. All he needed was her.

A bright yellow Kia drove under the motel sign. Lars pulled up the hood on his jacket and headed down the sidewalk toward her. He passed the car, then doubled back, staying out of her line of sight. By the time she realized he was there for her, he'd slammed her head into the steering wheel.

He pushed her into the passenger seat, then drove them to the location he'd set up for just this purpose. Oh, he wouldn't kill her right off. He'd give his dear sister an opportunity to save Sally. A man deserved some fun before he died, didn't he?

The abandoned barn sat well off the road. Lars heaved Sally onto his shoulders and went inside. He dumped her on a long folding table, then lit several oil lamps around the cavernous room in strategic places. The effect was exactly what he wanted. Light illuminated the body, dark as ink beyond. He rubbed his hands together and picked up a camera. Not a cell phone this time, but Luke's live news-cam. The only place receiving this particular feed would be his sister's phone.

"Hello, Sharlene. Behind me is the lovely Sally Suthers. I want to give you the chance to save her, so take a good look around the room. I'll take off pieces of this lovely lady until you find us. Oh, and I should mention, Sally is another of our father's offspring." He lifted the camera and scanned the inside of the barn, settling on Sally's body. "She'll be waking up within an hour or two. Then, the fun begins." He set the camera back on the tripod.

He moved to where he could stare into the lens. "Oh, and sis? Bring Dad and Candy when you come, would you?" He tied Sally to the table, then waited in the shadows for her to wake up.

Shar's phone vibrated across the coffee table. While Everis channel surfed for something to watch, she grabbed it before it landed on the floor. She glanced at the screen. A video from an unknown caller. The hair stood up on her arms as she pressed the button.

Lars's voice filled the room.

Everis leaned close to watch. "That's a barn."

"But where? This land is covered with barns." Her skin grew clammy. "He's going to torture this girl very slowly. He's flipped my plan of him coming to me. I have to figure out where he is and go to him, so she doesn't suffer too much." How many brothers and sisters did she have? Did no one practice birth control?

"I'm calling Mayfield and Pinson. We need all hands on deck." Everis reached for his phone. "That's a live feed. You may lose connection if you turn it off on your end."

Shar didn't bother changing this time. Nothing mattered but the woman tied to a six-foot folding table in a barn. As if from far away, she heard Everis ordering the deputies to come asap. While she watched, the woman—Sally, Lars had called her—opened her eyes.

Frightened, she glanced around her. "Hello?"

"Hello." Lars stepped back into view eating a sandwich. "So nice of you to agree to meet with me." He kicked a metal stool close to the table. "We're brother and sister, you and I. Oh, and the sheriff. She's our sister."

"What are you talking about?" Sally struggled against her bindings.

"We all share a father." He popped the last bite of the sandwich into his mouth and wiped his hands on his jeans before sitting down. "So, because we're related, I've decided not to kill you outright. Only little by little so our sheriff sister has time and opportunity to save you. I want us all to die together."

"Where are we?" Tears streamed down Sally's face.

Shar cried along with her.

"I don't want to spoil the live feed. Sheriff Shar needs to figure it out." He glanced at the camera. "Are you thinking hard, Sharlene?"

"Give me the phone." Everis held out his hand. "Let me watch."

Shar shook her head. "No. This woman is depending on me." She moved closer to Goliath, knowing the dog wouldn't let Everis get close if she didn't want him to. "Can we trace the camera?"

"I'll call the station." A few seconds later, he shook his head. "Luke Ball's camera was stolen. He preferred an older model. No way of tracing."

"Then how are we supposed to find this woman in time?" Shar shot to her feet, motioning for Goliath to stay down. "Oh, God, he has a knife."

Sally's screams ripped from the phone as Lars peeled a small section of skin from the back of her hand. Then, as her screams faded, he poured some kind of liquid on them, causing her screams to grow.

Shar's front door burst open.

Goliath charged.

Everis drew his gun.

Mayfield and Pinson, guns drawn, froze.

"What in the hell is going on here?" Pinson ordered.

"Put your guns away. The screams came from Sheriff Camenetti's phone." Everis set his weapon on the coffee table. "Lars Townsend is sending her a live feed of him torturing a woman. He's daring us to find out where he is and come save her."

They peered over Shar's shoulder.

"It's a barn," Pinson said.

"Of course, it's a barn." Shar wiped her arm across her eyes, hating that she felt the need to snap at him. "We need to know where it is. Deputy Mayfield, you grew up in these hills. Any idea?"

"It could be the one right off Stellar Road." He scrunched his mouth. "Of course, there's a big abandoned place off I-40. It could be almost anywhere,

Sheriff."

She turned to Everis. "Can you organize search parties to those areas while we think of more? We need all the help you can get us from Little Rock and beyond." She rushed into the kitchen and pulled a marker and a map of the area from the buffet drawer. After spreading the map on the kitchen table, she set the phone on the table next to it.

Using the marker, she circled the two places Mayfield had mentioned. A lot of space between the two circles. "Anyone know this woman's last name?"

Mayfield cleared his throat. "She's a uh, dancer, from Exposed."

Shar didn't want to know how he knew that. "Find out her name. I don't care about her occupation."

A quick phone call and they had the name of Sally Suthers. A quick driver's license search revealed the address. Shar donned her gun belt. "Let's go, boys."

"Uh, Sheriff." Everis grinned and pointed at her legs. "You going to wear those shorts?"

She rolled her eyes and dashed to her room for a pair of uniform pants. She grabbed her uniform shirt and cell phone on the way and rushed to her jeep. "Mayfield and Pinson, you follow us. Time is running out."

Chapter Nineteen

While Mayfield and Pinson headed back to the office to organize a search party, Shar, Everis, and Goliath headed to Sally Suthers's home. So many relatives within twenty minutes of each other, and most likely only the mothers knew. Surely the women knew Camenetti was seeing others. If life ever settled down enough, Shar would need days to process all the information and meet her half-siblings. Right now, a half-sister depended on her.

Suthers lived on the top floor of a two-story apartment building. Shar rang the bell to the manager's apartment and told him they needed into room 23. The man immediately rang them in and agreed to unlock the door.

A man Shar couldn't help but compare to the storybook character, Mr. Toad, met them on the landing in a forest-green robe and yellow slippers. Shar showed her identification.

"Ms. Suthers has never given us a lick of trouble. Always pays her rent on time. No male visitors. I can't imagine her having trouble with the law." He bustled ahead of them, a ring of keys jingling in his hand.

"Thank you, sir," Everis said, standing in the doorway. "We'll let you know if we need your further assistance."

The man tried peering around Everis, then shrugged. "I'll head back to bed, if you don't mind. Lock and close the door behind you."

The man seemed a bit put out. Shar shrugged. They had bigger things to worry about than an apartment manager's feelings. "This is a long shot," she said. "I doubt there will be anything here to tell us where Lars took Sally."

"I agree," Everis said. "But we can't rule it out."

Goliath entered first. Shar stood in the doorway and scanned the corners of the ceiling. "Camera top right."

"Got another one over the door."

"Which means he needs electricity where he is to run monitors." She bit her lower lip. "So why the lanterns? Effect?"

"That's my guess."

Shar didn't spot anymore cameras. Most likely Lars hadn't had the time. It was all part of his game. A search of the one-bedroom apartment didn't reveal anything of value other than the fact Sally and Lars had graduated together. That must have been a slam for him to find out he'd had a sister in his class. She replaced the yearbook in the bookcase as a voice from her cell phone began talking.

"Hey, sis, how ya doing?" Lars sat on the metal stool and smiled into the camera. "Sally hasn't had a luxurious life, but I was surprised at how clean her place was, considering she has a filthy job." He picked up a scalpel and ran the smooth side down Sally's cheek.

She whimpered and pulled away as far as her bindings would go. Her red-rimmed eyes stared into the camera. "Please, help me."

Shar wished she could speak to the woman, assure her she was doing everything in her power to find her. Give her promises she prayed she could keep.

Lars lifted the woman's hand and used a pair of pliers to pull out the teal-painted index finger of her left hand. Shrill screams filled the apartment. "I'm going to kill you, Lars." Whether he could hear or not, that was a promise she intended to keep. A lifetime of living on taxpayers' money was too good for him.

"Come on, Shar." Everis put his hand on the small of her back. "Let's join the others and find this woman before it's too late."

"It's already too late. She's already endured more than anyone should ever have to."

He guided her out the door and pulled it shut behind them. "If she's anything like you, she'll be strong enough to endure."

When they'd reached her jeep, he opened the passenger door. "I'll drive. You keep watching your phone."

Shar couldn't tear her eyes away. It had taken all her willpower to put her phone in her pocket when Sally had fallen asleep. Now that she was awake and hurting, Shar felt as if by watching, the woman could somehow feel as if she weren't alone.

*   *   *

"I'm quickly growing bored with you, sister." Lars clunked the handle of the pliers he'd used on the bleeding finger. "You need to scream more."

"I'm...not a screamer. Please."

"You'll scream plenty before I'm finished." He put the tool away and logged into the laptop on a small folding table. "We have lots more family members. I'd like to gather them all right here, then find dear old dad and make him pay for his infidelities. Wouldn't you like some company? The others are proving very hard to locate."

He drummed his fingers on his lips. "I bet they're written down somewhere. In the sheriff's office? Her home?" He could break into her home, but her office...He grabbed the keys to his car. "Don't go anywhere, Sally. I'll be back in an hour or so."

He knew no one worked at the department after hours. All calls were forwarded to an answering service who notified the sheriff of emergencies. If Lars were lucky, and he usually was, the place would be dark and locked down for the night.

It was. He stared through his windshield forty-five minutes later. It would be a cinch to get inside. After all, who but him wanted to break in?

He picked the door easily enough, and using nothing but a penlight on his keychain, made his way down the hall to the sheriff's office. He dared turning on the light, hoping the blinds wouldn't give away his presence.

Thumbing through a stack of papers, he found one with his father's name, a few women, some men, and a couple of question marks. He grinned. Sharlene was also searching. He wrote down the two men's names, then stared at the names of their mothers. Had their mothers loved them, or had they been looked upon in disgust as he had? Day after day, his mother had told him what a loser his father was, how he'd used her and tossed her aside, as if that had been Lars's fault.

He wasn't the one who'd slept with the devil. Deciding to leave the mothers be, he flicked off the light and headed back to his captive. He had plans to make and didn't want to leave her too long, unless the cavalry arrived.

While he drove, he worked to find a way to get a post office worker and another man who delivered water to come to him. Setting up a fake address would take too much time. He tapped his fingers on the steering wheel.

The only way he could figure was to grab each man during his deliveries. Which meant time watching their routine. Time he wasn't sure he had. If Sally wasn't discovered soon, he'd have to start giving her food and water.

Everis stepped into the sheriff department, his eyes fixed on the floor. Footsteps marred the freshly-mopped tiles. "Shar."

"Yeah." She entered the building, followed by the two deputies.

"Someone has been inside." He glanced around the room, pulling his weapon from its holster. "The back door is ajar."

"Who would be stupid enough to break in?" Pinson scowled. "Do they want to go to jail?"

"It had to be Lars," Shar said. "He hasn't been on the video for more than an hour." She hurried to her office. "He's been in here. That stack of papers is moved."

"What's missing?" Everis put his weapon away. There wasn't anywhere to hide, and Lars would have no reason to hang around.

"Nothing." She frowned. "I think the page with the sibling names isn't exactly where I'd left it in the stack, but I can't be sure."

"We need to warn them." Everis hurried to the reception desk, sat in the large chair they'd found for Atilla the Hun and searched for the men's phone numbers. He scribbled them on a sheet of paper, then called both men, waking them up, and asked that they come to the department immediately. They both said they'd be there within ten minutes. Two men were about to get a big surprise.

He glanced up when Shar joined him. Lines marred her beautiful face. The case was wearing her down. He wanted to ease her burden more than anything. He couldn't imagine discovering a half-brother was a serial killer with a vengeance against every member of his family.

"Where are we on the search parties?" Shar asked.

"Gathering at first light right outside," Mayfield said. "We sent alerts out to every phone number we had."

Everis didn't grow up in small-town country, but if this town was like ones he'd heard about, they'd have a horde outside willing to help. He logged off the computer and motioned for Shar to follow him. "Send the men in to the conference room," he told Mayfield.

He flipped the case board over to hide its contents and sat down to wait. "What a way to find out they have a sister."

Shar raised her eyebrows. "Shocking." She stiffened as both Mark Arnes and Ben Wilson stepped into the room.

"Sit down, gentlemen." Everis motioned to the chairs across the table from them. "What the sheriff has to say will come as quite a shock to you. Please don't ask questions until she's finished."

Their attention focused on Shar.

She sighed and set her phone to silent. "Gentlemen, there is no other way to say this, but we share the same father. Robert Camenetti has left a trail of offspring across this county, one of which is Lars Townsend, aka The Silencer." She held up a hand when Arnes started to speak. "We've called you in here because we have reason to believe that your lives are in danger."

"We're related to you?" Arnes frowned, then jerked his thumb in the direction of Wilson. "And each other? And a killer?"

"Welcome to the family, boys."

"Is this why you visited my mother a few days ago?" Arnes glanced between them. "Is this why we had to provide DNA?"

"Yes to both." Everis folded his hands on the table and leaned forward. "I realize this isn't the best way for family to find out about each other, but we have no choice. Lars Townsend has your names and knows you are his half-brothers. He's vowed to take all of you down with him."

"Why?" Wilson finally spoke. "We've done nothing to him. We aren't responsible for who our parents are."

"At least you didn't grow up thinking the man who raised you was your father?" Arnes glared.

"How do you know that?" Wilson stood. "I've always known my father left my mother when I was born."

"Before." Mark grinned. "Get 'em pregnant and dump 'em."

Shar slapped her hands on the table. "Mr. Arnes. Mr. Wilson. We are concerned for your very lives. At this moment, Lars is holding our half-sister, Sally Suthers, as captive and is torturing her." She pulled out her phone and turned the screen, so they could see. "It's on a live feed. Do you know what's it like to hear her scream?"

They paled and shook their heads.

Shar raised the volume, filling the room with pain and fear. "This woman, whether you want to accept it or not, is your sister. She is going to die. The killer is going to come after you. I need you to stop acting like children and cooperate."

"How?" Arnes wiped his hands repeatedly on the leg of his pants.

"Pack a bag and get out of here. Don't tell anyone where you're going. Not your parents, girlfriend, work…no one. Lars is a shrewd predator. If you leave a trail, he will find you."

Chapter Twenty

Volunteers from surrounding towns congregated in front of the sheriff's office. A spark of hope ignited in Shar's chest. They might find Sally after all. Mark and Ben still seemed a bit shell-shocked when they left that morning. Shar had insisted they not tell her where they were going, only that they leave their phone numbers.

Everis divided the thirty or so men into groups, each group accompanied by no less than two police officers, also volunteering to search on their day off. He then handed each group a map with their area circled. "Leave no building unsearched, and use extreme caution. Lars Townsend is considered very dangerous."

The understatement of the year. The man was psychotic.

Shar stepped off the steps, ignoring Everis's glare. There was absolutely no way she was staying at the office while the others searched. She'd be safe enough with Everis glued to her side. She met his stare and smiled. There was no one better to watch her back.

"Sheriff." Mayfield jogged to her side. "Pinson and I are going with the folks from Hollow Ridge if you think Agent Hayes is enough backup for you."

"He's enough. We need to as much ground as much as possible." She spread the map across the hood of her jeep and studied the area she'd be searching. Sneaky. Everis had circled the thick woods and mountain behind her house. One way or another the man thought he could keep her down. She grabbed Mayfield's map. "Trade."

He shrugged and headed back to the others while Shar unfolded the new map. She grinned. They were ten miles out of town and in thick woods. The only way in and out was a rutted dirt road.

Everis yelled for everyone to hit the road.

Shar climbed into the driver's seat as the first of the sun's rays peeked over the mountain, turning low-hanging clouds the color of pumpkin. Once Everis joined her, she turned north and headed toward Missouri.

"This is the wrong way." Everis cut her a glance.

"Not according to the map on the dash."

He grabbed it and unfolded it. "You switched. I swear you have a death wish." He tossed the map back on the dash. "We are now headed into the densest forest surrounding Highland Springs with five city slickers following in a van like a bunch of soccer moms."

She laughed. "If I were holding someone hostage, I'd want dense forest."

"It's not funny."

Her laugh faded. "You're right. It isn't. That's why you need to stop mothering me and let me do my job." She handed Everis her phone. "He hasn't been back all night. Sally has woken several times, cried out, but if he's there, he's stayed out of camera sight."

"That can't be good."

"I agree."

Almost passing the road, Shar whipped the jeep to

the right and watched through the rearview mirror as the following van did the same. They hadn't gone fifty yards before the road became impassable for the van. She should have insisted on searchers with four-wheel drives. She cut the engine and stepped onto a muddy path. Sloshing to the back of the jeep, she pulled out a rifle, a raincoat, and another handgun. "We're going to get wet." She tossed another raincoat to Everis, then donned hers and slapped a wide-brimmed hat on her head.

"It would have been too much to hope for clear skies." He donned the coat and waved the others forward. "Keep conversation to a minimum. Divide into pairs, each pair with a radio. If you spot something, do not, I repeat do not advance. Call me or the sheriff and wait for us to join you. We don't need any heroes today."

The volunteers branched off heading into the trees. Shar led Everis further down the road. She scanned the trees on each side of them. "I don't see any electrical wires," she said, keeping her voice low.

"He could have a generator and a hotspot on his phone. Townsend will have thought of every scenario." Everis pushed a branch away from their faces and ducked.

"True." They were searching every known area that had a barn, no matter how dilapidated. Some areas had more than one. It never failed to surprise her that people preferred to let barns fall into ruin rather than tear them down. She glanced at her phone.

Rain dripped onto Sally. She shifted her head back and forth in a vain attempt to keep it out of her face. Lars was dishing out a new form of torture. "If you're out there, Sheriff, please help me. I don't know when he's coming back. I can't take anymore." She sobbed, her face crumbling. "He's been gone all night. What if he's leaving me to starve?"

Shar hadn't thought of that. Was it possible Lars only threatened to slowly kill Sally by his hand or was his intention to let the lack of food and water do it for him over time? It had been two days. Had he given Sally anything to drink before leaving?

"What are you thinking?" Everis put a hand on her shoulder and peered under her hat. "You wouldn't have stopped walking for no reason. What's up?"

"I think he's left her die on her own." Chills that had nothing to do with the rain skittered up her spine. "We're getting close to the cabin where my family is."

"You think he's gone there? They're miles away."

"He won't stop looking. With time, if he knows the area, he could stumble across them."

Everis's radio crackled. "Agent, we found a cabin with footprints and tire tracks."

"On our way. Hold your position. We'll be there in thirty minutes."

Together, they raced back to the jeep, instructing the others to keep looking in case of a false alarm.

* * *

He hated rain. How was a man to hide if he left tracks everywhere he went? Lars huddled behind some bushes and watched as five imbeciles circled the cabin he'd called home for the last week. They'd discover signs of him, but nothing of dear Sally. No, she was miles from there.

Lars started to melt into the shadows when Shar and the agent raced toward the group. Look at her!

Marvelous. Long legs, intelligent eyes in a beautiful face. He almost wished they weren't related. He'd like Sharlene for much more than a sister.

He couldn't hear what they discussed, not with the patter of rain on leaves, but he imagined they spoke of his brilliance. How he kept outsmarting them. He would be a killer for the history books.

Not wanting to risk exposure, Lars backed away.

A twig snapped to his left. Everis whirled, reaching for his gun. He stepped in front of Shar as calmly as possible and studied the tree line. When no more sounds came, he chalked the noise off to an animal. Then why did his skin prickle?

Keeping an eye on the surrounding woods, Everis stayed between Shar and whoever might be watching. Being overly cautious had saved his life more than once. He didn't dismiss that feeling of uneasiness.

"Let's go." Shar headed for the cabin, Everis right next to her.

Weapons drawn, they stepped back as another law enforcement officer kicked in the door. No explosions. No gunshots. No screams.

With his back to the wall, Everis peered around the corner. No Sally. In fact, the place was almost bare. He stepped inside, taking in the cot and sleeping bag, camping stove, and box of canned goods. It was clear someone had been living there. Townsend? He glanced back outside.

"What is it?" Shar asked.

"I think someone was watching us from the woods." He clenched his fists. They could have been mere feet from Townsend. If so, why hadn't he attempted to take

Shar? A few well-placed bullets and she would have been his for the taking. "Everyone out of the cabin. We need to keep it as clean as possible for forensics."

Another call on his radio soon had him and Shar speeding in the opposite direction. As the crow flies, the second cabin was maybe a mile. On poorly-graded dirt roads, it was ten.

Mayfield greeted them. "We called out and got an answer. Suthers is inside. Pinson is talking to her from a few feet away."

"Tell me you've called an ambulance," Shar said marching toward the cabin.

"On its way."

"Good job." Everis clapped the deputy on the shoulder and followed Shar. "Don't barge in. It could be a trap."

Pinson stood at the bottom of the two steps that led to the open door of the cabin. Inside, a tear-stained face stared back at them. "She's fine, other than weak and frightened," he said.

Shar nodded and moved forward. "Is there anyone in there with you, Sally?"

"No."

"Are there any traps that you know of?"

"I don't think so." Sally glanced around the room.

"I'll go in first." Everis stepped around Shar.

"He won't blow the building up," she said. "The whole family isn't here." She pushed past him and inside.

"Stubborn woman." Everis followed her, studying the room around them. Very little oil remained in the lanterns. By nightfall, Sally would have been in the dark. A camera on a tripod filmed as Shar knelt beside her newly-found sister. Everis reached over and turned it off. "Somebody, bag that for evidence."

He cut the bindings away from Sally's wrists and ankles, then helped Shar ease her off the table. "Take it easy. Your legs won't want to hold you."

"Thank you so much for finding me." She choked on a sob. "I thought I was going to die. He said we were all related. Is that true?"

"I'm afraid so." Shar gave a shaky grin. "Let's get you taken care of, and then I'll explain everything."

They helped her outside. The ambulance pulled as close to the cabin as possible. While the paramedics loaded Sally inside, Everis called off the search.

He headed to where he'd heard the twig snap. He had to know whether it was an animal they sought. He knelt beside a ten-and-a-half-foot print in the mud. He picked up a rock and threw it against the nearest tree. So close. Animal was too good a term for Townsend.

"Can you hear me, Townsend? You aren't going to win. We know you're dying. If we don't catch you, we'll keep chasing you until you can't run anymore."

"Try me, agent." Lar's voice came from his right. "I could shoot you here, now, but my grievance isn't against you."

Everis moved toward the sound. "Sheriff Camenetti has done nothing wrong. You're a killer."

"Yes, I am. The sheriff's only fault is having not grown up alone."

"Not her fault." Everis kept moving.

The rustle of bushes drew him to the left. "Let's get you medical attention, Townsend. Maybe we can prolong your life."

"In prison. No, that's very kind of you, but I'll die

along with my family." Pounding footsteps spurred Everis into a run.

He followed the sound of thrashing and breaking branches. Behind him, he heard the heavy breathing of Shar. No surprise there. She most likely followed the moment she noticed him missing.

"I'll veer right," she said, heading off, gun drawn.

"Don't leave my sight." Everis veered left.

Minutes later, they burst onto a dirt road and caught a glimpse of taillights disappearing over the hill. Shar rubbed her hands down her face and took several deep breaths. "At least we found Sally."

"We'll get him, too."

She glanced up. "You didn't promise that time."

"What?" He held out his hand to her.

She stepped back. "You always promise. You've lost hope."

Had he? "I've chased this man for so long, but I've never been this close. Then, he's gone again." He dropped his hand. "Yeah, I can't make that promise anymore. This might be a killer who dies without justice served." If that happened, Everis would walk away from being an agent. What kind of agent gets within feet of a perp and doesn't realize it?

"Don't say that. I've held on to your promise. Don't take that away."

He locked gazes with her pleading one. "Okay, Shar. I promise." What if he couldn't keep it?

Chapter Twenty-One

Shar knew he couldn't keep that type of vow, but not hearing him say the words was like a stab in the gut. She'd held onto the hope they would catch Lars. Seeing the hopeless look on Everis's face made her doubt their abilities. She glanced at the leaving ambulance. But, they had saved a life.

"Now what, boss?" Mayfield asked.

"We keep looking for Lars. He'll have to find another out-of-the-way place to stay. Convene at the office in thirty." She moved back to Everis's side. "We need men to watch every motel within a thirty-mile radius. A tall order, I know."

"We'll plaster his face on television again. Someone will see him." He headed for the jeep.

Shar heaved a sigh and hurried after him. "I'm sorry."

"For what?" He glanced across the hood of the jeep.

"Making you promise. I know you can't."

They didn't speak on the way back to the office by way of the coffee shop. After a long morning, Shar knew her team needed something other than what their receptionist made. She also bought a dozen assorted muffins. When she returned to the jeep, Everis wasn't inside.

She set the coffee and box of muffins on the hood

of the jeep and glanced up and down the street. Where could he have gone? Surely, he hadn't walked back to the office. She eyed the sky. The earlier rain had stopped, but the pregnant clouds looked ready to give birth to a doozy of a downpour any minute.

She moved the drinks and food into the back of the jeep and secured the coffee so it wouldn't spill. circle the block and see if she could spot him.

He flagged her down outside the newspaper office. "Sorry. I spotted the cameraman heading here and wanted to ask him whether he had any ideas where Lars might hold up."

"Does he?"

Everis shook his head. "No. Nobody does. They say Lars minded his own business, did his job, and was punctual. Nothing that helps us one bit."

"Those are the same questions and answers Mayfield got once we knew the identity of the killer." She steered them back toward the office. "Were you hoping for something different?"

"Luke spent part of most days with Lars. I'd hoped he might have picked up on something through his camera lens. Nope. He said the world looks different through a lens, and he was focused on the story."

Idiot. "We're grasping at straws." She parked in her usual spot and retrieved the drinks and muffins as the clouds opened. Everis grabbed the drinks and sprinted for the building, Shar close on his heels.

Once inside, she shook the rain from her hair. "He'll come to us."

"What makes you so positive? He wants everyone together. He won't come until that happens."

"Then, we make him think they're here." She

headed for the conference room. "Pinson can dress like my father, and Mayfield can slap on a dark wig to look like Candy. We'll sit around the kitchen table enjoying dinner and wait for him to show up."

"Why do I have to dress up like Candy?" Mayfield peered into the bag. "Yum, orange spice."

"Because I won't." Pinson grabbed a multi-grain. "Besides, you've got a prettier face."

"Shut up." Mayfield threw a muffin wrapper at him.

"Settle down, boys." Shar took her seat at the head of the table. "You'll also have to sleep at my place. If Lars is watching, he'll know whether the light in Candy's room flicks on and whether someone is staying in my guest room."

Everyone groaned except Everis who looked deep in thought. "I don't think we'll fool him."

"Why not?" Shar crossed her arms.

"He's been studying your family for a very long time. He knows what your father looks like, how he moves. Same with your sister."

"What if we station officers outside, so he can't get close enough to get a good look?"

He shrugged and sat next to her. "Anything is worth a try. We can use some of the men left from the morning's search."

Shar pressed her lips together and watched as Everis focused on the pencil he twirled between his fingers. She saw defeat in every line of his face, the slump of his shoulders. "Deputies, please allow Agent Hayes and myself some privacy."

All three men glanced at her in surprise, but the deputies left, closing the door behind them. Everis smirked. "Are you going to lecture me, Sheriff?"

"Do you know why I got this job?"

He shook his head.

"Because my stepfather was a respected man of this community. He was the sheriff before me. When he passed, shortly after I completed training and returned to Highland Springs, I was asked to run for the position. It was a unanimous vote."

He narrowed his eyes. "Why are you telling me this?"

"Because, even though I was asked to take this position, I struggle with my ineptness every single day."

"It's not the same thing."

"Isn't it?" She moved to his side of the table and perched on the edge. "You're feeling as if you're not good enough to catch Lars. You've been chasing him for over a year. Now, you're this close…" she held her fingers an inch apart, "and he slipped away. I think it's exactly the same, Everis." She cupped his face. "You're a good agent. I'm a good sheriff. We're human."

He gave a lopsided smile. "Are you going to remember those words the next time you're feeling inadequate?"

"I sure am going to try." She straightened. "Let's go catch this bastard. You have a promise to keep."

Everis admired Shar's attempt to cheer him up. She was right. If they failed to catch Lars, it had nothing to do with Everis's abilities, but rather on Lars's skill. Still, Everis wanted to take the man down more than he'd wanted anything in his life.

Shar opened the door for the deputies to join them. "We'll have to get you to my house under pretense.

Dark van, hooded jackets, etc. We want him to believe it's my family. Any questions?"

"Are you a good cook or are we eating takeout while we wait?" Pinson leaned back in his chair.

Everis laughed. "She's a good cook."

Thunder rumbled overhead, loud enough to rattle windows.

"This is as good a time as any. A downpour will make it hard for him to spot your true identities."

"What about our uniforms?" Mayfield glanced at his lap. "We need street clothes."

"I've got something that might fit you." Everis stood. "Pinson?"

"I've a pair of jeans in my locker."

"Convene back here in fifteen." Everis gave Shar a nod, then went to alert the receptionist that all calls were to be forwarded to the sheriff's private cell phone.

"Why?"

"Because we'll be operating out of her house for now."

"Why?" The woman's eyes disappeared under her lowered brow. "Does this mean I'm no longer needed?"

"Her family has returned, and yes, I do believe your services are no longer needed. Thank you." He grinned.

She struggled to her feet. "Make sure and give me a good referral." She shouldered her purse and ambled out the back door.

He'd give her a referral, alright.

Right on time, they gathered in front of the main doors, ready to dash to a waiting van. Shar would drive herself while Everis rode in the van, on the pretense of guarding the occupants. Something he was not happy about. He should be driving her precious jeep, thus keeping Shar in the van where it was safer.

By the time they arrived at her home, the rain came down in torrents, a more effective cover than the dark was. Everis didn't put it past Lars to have night-vision goggles. Not much one could see through a downpour like this.

Enveloped in raincoats and umbrellas, the group trooped up the steps and through Shar's front door where Goliath ran around in circles. Shar knelt down and wrapped her arms around his neck. "I'm sorry, fella. We've been running around to places I couldn't bring you. It's almost over."

Everis circled the house, making sure the blinds were closed. With the men stationed outside, the blinds drawn, and Goliath prowling the house, Lars would have to be extra talented to get close. Their only chance of fooling him was if he saw the group leave the van and enter the house.

"Are you sure this place isn't bugged?" Pinson surveyed the living room. "Because there's enough girlie doo-dads to hide one."

"This is...was...my mother's house. I haven't had the heart to change anything." Shar headed for the kitchen. "Candy's room is the yellow one at the top of the stairs. The guest room is downstairs, end of the hall." She grinned at Mayfield. "You look nice with long hair."

He growled and flopped onto the sofa. Soon, he idly flicked through television channels. "This better work. My head itches."

Pinson sat next to him, so close he was almost on Mayfield's lap. "Hey, gorgeous. Where you been all my life?"

Mayfield planted his hands on the man's chest and shoved. "Get off me before I shoot you."

Everis laughed and followed Shar into the kitchen. "Tweedle-Dee and Tweedle-Dum seem to be getting along."

"Yeah." She pulled a pie out of the freezer. "Pinson still sulks about having to work for a woman, but at least he doesn't balk every time I tell him to do something."

"He'll come around. Is that homemade?"

"Cherry, and yes. I made several and froze them for times like this."

He grinned and leaned against the counter, facing her. "Times when you're hiding in your home with several men from your brother?"

"Hush. You know what I mean." Her cheeks darkened.

"Can I kiss you again?"

Her eyes widened. "You're asking?"

"Well, I wasn't sure how you felt about the others knowing about us."

She shook her head. "There is no us, Everis. You'll be leaving, and I'm not into long-distance relationships."

"Two hours. I could come here every weekend."

"It wouldn't—" She motioned to Goliath.

The dog's hackles were raised as he stared at the back door.

"Get back. Alert the others."

Everis approached the backdoor, one hand on his weapon.

* * *

Lars pressed against the wall of the house as Agent

Hayes peered out the curtains. When the doorknob started to turn, he slipped around the corner.

He'd seen the van pull up and release its passengers. Glee had risen so fast he'd laughed out loud. They'd come. His family had arrived. Shar was even preparing pie for them. He would join them for dessert, then take them to death along with himself.

He tiptoed across the front porch, familiar now with where the squeaky boards were. A slit in the front blinds provided a view of his no-good father. Taking his time, he slid along the wall an inch at a time, stopping at regular intervals to listen.

No cries of alarm. No barks. No gunshots. No one knew he was there.

He rubbed his hands together and swiveled to peek through the slit between the blinds and came face-to-face with a set of dark brown eyes. No one in his family had brown eyes.

A man yelled out. "He's here!"

Lars leaped off the porch as the front door swung open. He rolled under a vehicle and out the other side as shots were fired.

They'd tried tricking him. Now, they would have to pay. He'd bring his family home, and he knew exactly how to accomplish that.

Keeping low, he darted into the woods as shouts and thundering feet followed. Good luck, gentlemen. Can't catch me.

Lars jumped over an incline, slid down a ravine, and splashed through a creek. Soon, the only sound was his breathing and the pitter-patter of raindrops on tree leaves. He'd escaped again.

Chapter Twenty-Two

Shar called Goliath to heel and stared down the ravine. She aimed her weapon just as Lars dashed into the shadows.

"Again." Everis pounded his fist on his thigh. "The man is a ghost. A wisp of smoke, there one minute, gone the next."

"Let's head back. We can't shoot something we can't see." She wanted to wring Pinson's neck, the fool. Peering through the blinds had alerted Lars. She marched to the house and barged through the front door.

"You." She poked Pinson in the chest. "What were you doing peeking outside like a child waiting for Santa Claus? He recognized you, and now he's gone. You're an imbecile." She closed her eyes and took a deep breath. "I'm sorry. I'm out of line. You're free to go home. I'll see you in the office in the morning." With her hand on Goliath's head, she headed to her room.

On the bed, she dangled her hand over the side, resting it on the dog's head. She regretted her outburst. Of course, Pinson would look outside to see who was sneaking around. To lose Lars again…she knew exactly how Everis had felt over the last year.

Shar woke to rattling windows and Goliath's whimpers. An orange glow filled the sky outside her window.

Everis burst into her room as she swung her legs over the bed. "There's been an explosion. Mayfield said it's the sheriff's office. How soon can you be ready?"

She swallowed against the mountain in her throat. "Now. I slept in my clothes. Goliath, stay." Grabbing her shoulder holster on the way, she rushed out the front door with Everis. "Anyone injured?"

"We don't know yet."

By the time they arrived in front of the inferno that was once the sheriff's office, firemen worked frantically to keep the flames from spreading to adjacent buildings. No one needed to tell her that Lars was responsible. He had a reason for blowing up her office, but what?

Staying out of the way, she made a wide circle of the building and studied the alley in back. A gas can and a candlelighter lay in the middle of a parking space. Lars hadn't tried to hide the fact the fire was arson.

"What are you looking for?" Everis joined her.

"Why blow up the building?" She glanced up to see the news van. A woman in a suit climbed out. "It looks like they've replaced Lars with an Amazon." The woman had to be six-feet without her heels.

She strode toward them. "I'm Sue Lincoln, the new reporter. You must be Sheriff Camenetti." She gave a closed-lipped smile. The woman wasn't pretty by any means, but she did command a presence.

"Yes." She thrust out her hand. "Nice to meet you. As you can see, we're very busy at the moment."

"Anything you can tell me?"

"We suspect the fire was started by Lars Townsend. That's all. Please excuse me." Shar forced a smile and continued down the alley, scanning the ground for further clues. She found nothing. Instead, she turned to see Sue and Luke filming the fire live. It would be on everyone's television within fifteen minutes.

"That woman is a tyrant." Everis glared. "I told her no filming, she gave me the freedom-of-speech spiel, then told Luke to start filming, and if I didn't want to be on camera denying her rights, I'd best step back."

"It doesn't matter."

"It does. Townsend thrives on the attention."

"We need to find out his reason for torching this place." She headed back to the front of the building. The news team followed. Great. She was out of uniform, hair hanging down, and on the news. She reached up and twisted her hair into a lopsided knot. People would have to understand that the sheriff didn't sleep in her uniform. The oversized tee shirt and short shorts didn't help her image any, though. She waved Mayfield over. "Find me some pants."

"I've an extra pair in my truck." He jogged off, returning with uniform pants and a shirt.

Shar donned them over the clothes she wore and surveyed the crowd. He was here, watching. She felt him. The evilness hung over the area like a heavy cloud, malevolent and vicious. The time for them to come face-to-face for a final showdown was creeping closer.

"Where are we going to have our base of operations now?" Pinson stood next to her and crossed his arms. Leave it to him to worry more about work than people.

"We'll figure it out. Do they know yet whether or not the building was vacant?"

"It was."

"I guess we'll hold office in my place until we find something else."

She could feel him. He could see it in the way she scanned the crowd. Lars pulled his hat lower across his eyes and became one with the block wall behind him. Act as if you belonged, and people thought you did. He'd learned that shortly after taking his first victim. Of course, then, he'd been behind a microphone.

Things weren't as easy anymore. Everyone was looking for him. Anyone who spotted him would squeal. He'd taken a great risk coming to watch his sister's reaction. Seeing the determination on her face, the way the people of Highland Springs catered to her, it was all worth it. Now to wait and see whether his plan would work. He gave a jaunty salute in Sharlene's direction, then strode down the sidewalk, whistling as if he didn't have a care in the world.

By the time the fire was out, the crowd dispersed, and the scene cased, Shar was more than ready to head home. Exhaustion weighed her shoulders, despite the three cups of coffee she'd drunk. As long as someone thrust one in her hands, she drank. The sun had risen an hour ago, and the day promised to be hot.

She rubbed her hands up and down her face, then called to Everis and the deputies to meet at her house. She'd whip up something for them to eat, then formulate a new case board on the kitchen wall.

"I'll drive." Everis snatched the keys from her hand. "You look like you're ready to fall over."

"I am. Thanks." She gladly relinquished the right to drive. Closing her eyes, even for the few-minutes drive outside of town, would relieve some of the tiredness.

"Uh-oh."

Shar's eyes snapped open at Everis's muttering. "What?"

"Company."

She sat up in her seat. "What the heck are they doing here?" She flung open her door and marched through the front door. "Robert. Candy. You are not supposed to be here." She glared at each in turn, settling on Natalie. "You're the authority."

"They started to leave when I was in the bathroom." Natalie held up her hands. "Once they saw the sheriff's office had blown up, nothing would stop them."

Shar spun back to her father and froze. This is why Lars blew up the office. "He wanted this. He has us all in one place."

"What do we do now?" Her father came from the kitchen, a frying pan in his hand. "I'm cooking breakfast, although I didn't expect so many people. What do we do when we've finished eating?"

Shar looked to Everis for help. The thought of them remaining together, even for the short time it would take to eat, scared her senseless. If Lars were to blow up the house, there was nothing any of them could do. "You have to get out of here. Candy, talk some sense into him."

Her sister shrugged from her seat on the sofa. "He won't listen." She pretended to study her nails, while peeking at Pinson from under lowered lashes. "Said we should be together at a time like this."

"That's the worst thing possible. Ugh." Shar stormed to her room and slammed the door. Maybe Everis could talk sense into the hard-headed

Camenettis.

She changed into her own uniform and tossed the borrowed one into the clothes hamper. She might be working out of her home, but she was working and needed to look the part. Squaring her shoulders, she headed back to the living room to face her family.

"Mr. Camenetti," Everis was saying, "you've put everyone in danger by being here. I guarantee Townsend knows you're here and is watching the house at this moment. We need to get you somewhere safe."

"I'm not going anywhere without my girls. Both of them." He slid an omelet onto a plate and handed it to Everis. "I wasn't much of a father, which is why we're in this mess. I won't desert them now."

Shar slipped her mask into place. "You're going to get us killed. Being a father is too little, too late."

"He's trying, Shar." Candy dropped her feet from the coffee table and stood. "We're all stressed, we're all frightened, so we might as well be together."

Shar frowned. "Don't you get it? Are none of you listening?"

Everis put a hand on her shoulder. "You can't make them do something they don't want to do. Come on. Let's eat."

"You could arrest them and take them to a neighboring city until this over," Pinson suggested. "For their own good, you know."

"I can't believe I thought you handsome." Candy brushed past him.

What was happening here? Shar had lost complete control. "We're going to split up, ride in separate vehicles, and follow Deputy Pinson's advice. We're getting out of here."

Everis did his best to herd the others. Candy would ride with him and Shar. Robert would ride with the two deputies. He didn't hold out a lot of faith in the idea working, but Shar was right. They couldn't stay there together. The only thing keeping them alive was separation. "We'll go to the federal office in Little Rock. They'll be safe there." Unless Lars could turn into smoke and go through the ventilation system.

Shar again agreed to ride shotgun. "Keep your wits about you, people. Lars is going to act while we're on the road. I guarantee it."

Everis feared she was right. But how? Roadblock? Trap? Neither would be good for the Camenettis. He wished they had time to call for an escort.

He climbed into the driver's seat and drove to the interstate. It was going to be a long, stress-filled drive. Already the muscles in his shoulders were tensing up. His knuckles turned white from his tight grip on the steering wheel. He glanced repeatedly in the rearview mirror.

"Geez, Agent." Candy smacked his shoulder. "Relax. You're making everybody nervous."

"You should be nervous." He tossed a glance over his shoulder.

"Look out!" Shar whipped the steering wheel from his hands. They narrowly missed a spike strip stretched across their lane and stopped on the grassy shoulder.

The other guy wasn't so lucky. Tires screeched behind them as they veered toward the ditch. Mayfield's car hit the culvert turning the front end into an accordion.

Shar flung open her door. "Stay down, Candy. Lock

the doors." She raced for the other car.

Everis stayed close on her heels. The back of his neck prickled. Where would the threat come from? The other side of the street? This one? From behind them?

Shar fought to get the truck door open. The airbags had deployed, making it impossible. "Use the back window. Break it out."

Everis climbed into the bed of the truck and shattered the window with a tire iron. "You'll have to squeeze through here, Camenetti."

"Impossible." The man eyed the hole.

"There's no other way unless you want to crawl through the front window glass."

"I choose that." He waited while the deputies climbed out, then followed.

Everis whirled as a gun cocked. "Get down!"

A shot rang out from the trees.

Camenetti dove in front of him. The shot took him in the chest. Blood stained the front of the old man's shirt.

A curse came from the trees.

Someone screamed.

Everis, Shar, and the deputies aimed for the forest and fired.

Chapter Twenty-Three

"See to your father," Everis said, not taking his eyes off the trees or his finger off the trigger. "We got this. Lars won't shoot you or Candy."

Shar nodded and rushed to where her sister knelt next to their father. Robert turned his head and held out his hand to her. Shar wrapped it in her own.

"This is it, girls," he said. "I'm not getting out of this one."

Tears blurred Shar's eyes. Anger from her father's past mistakes had clouded her vision and robbed her of the short time they could have had together. "I'm sorry...Dad."

"Yeah, me too." He closed his eyes for a moment. "Take care of your man, Sharlene."

"You took a bullet for him."

"It would have gone through him and hit you." He crooked his mouth. "My last act as a father. Hell, probably my only act."

"Don't say that." Candy lifted his other hand to her mouth as sirens screamed in the distance. "We'll get you to the hospital. You'll be fine. It's just a flesh wound."

Shar glanced at where the blood bubbled from his chest. It didn't take a doctor to see that her father wasn't going to live much longer. She was so intent on his face, she didn't notice when Everis put his hand on her shoulder until he squeezed. The shooting had stopped. Mayfield and Pinson were nowhere to be seen.

"He's gone, sweetheart."

"Lars?"

"No, your father." He pulled her up and into his arms. "I owe him my life."

"We both do." She leaned her forehead against his chest and took a deep shuddering breath. "Who knew he was capable of such an unselfish action? I was so very mean to him."

He cupped her face and tilted her to look at him. "Please, don't think any of this is your fault. We're all responsible for the choices we make in life." He planted a kiss on her lips. "Let's case the scene and get your father's body taken care of."

She turned and saw Candy sitting alone, her back against the jeep, looking sadder than she'd ever seemed. The dejection shattered her heart so loudly she heard the pieces fall to the ground. Almost forty-years-old or not, Candy had always wished for their father to return.

Shar sat next to her and took her sister's hand. They sat there, unspeaking, while the ME van took their father's body away. By the time he was gone, and the scene cased, dusk had started to fall. Another day where Lars still walked the earth.

* * *

No! Lars sped down the highway. Nothing was going according to plan. He'd meant to kill the agent, not his father. His plans were ruined.

He pounded the steering wheel and cursed. Fire burned through his groin. His head pounded. He'd barely made it out of the gunfight alive, but every minute that passed, his strength ebbed. He had to stay alive long enough to take his sisters with him.

He pulled into a gas station on the side of the highway and tugged a baseball cap low on his head. After filling the car with fuel, he filled a five-gallon gas can. He'd need it for later.

If he knew his sisters, which he thought he did, they'd follow dear old dad's body to the morgue. That's where the next phase of his plan would take place. He laughed, then hunched his shoulders in case anyone might be suspicious of a lone man laughing to himself.

After carefully stashing the plastic can in the trunk of his car, he pulled out the pump, paid via credit card, and sped away. There was probably an alert on his card. Shar would know within minutes that he'd used it and where. It wouldn't matter. She already knew he was after her.

He parked under a low-hanging branch on the far side of the hospital parking lot and waited. Sure enough, he'd guessed right. Shar and Candy pulled up to the morgue, deputies following. Strange. Usually the agent rode with his sisters. Where was the man?

* * *

Everis shined his flashlight across the ground. There was where Townsend had lain in wait. He bent and studied the imprint of a knee, where the toes of his shoe had dug into the dirt. He straightened and glanced toward the road. Lars had had a perfect sight line.

If he'd wanted Everis dead, then he and Shar were getting too close for comfort. What would he do now that he'd killed his father? Was that part of the man's psychotic plan? Everis didn't think so.

He glanced to where flattened grass and broken

branches showed the way Townsend had fled. Everis followed the path, eventually coming out on a poor excuse for a dirt road. For someone who hadn't lived his whole life in Highland Springs, the man knew his way around.

Too well. He had to be hiding somewhere close. Within five miles would be Everis's guess.

He circled around slowly. A five-mile radius covered a lot of ground. They needed to search from the ground. If they didn't find him within five miles, they'd go ten. They would find him. Everis had a promise to uphold.

He unclipped his radio from his belt and radioed for a chopper.

"I can't believe he's gone." Candy covered her face with her hands.

Shar let go of the door to the morgue and let it close. "Me neither. Even though he wasn't in our lives, he was here, living not far from us." Making babies, drinking beer, living off unemployment when he wasn't tending bar. Yeah, she'd kept track of him, despite not wanting to.

"We're orphans." She lifted tear-reddened eyes. "I know that sounds childish at our age, but we really are now. No parents, no lover, just us two."

"That's not true. Mark and Ben, remember? Sally? We just need to have a...family reunion." Shar forced a smile. "Don't forget our psycho brother, Lars."

"Yes, please don't forget him."

Shar froze and slowly turned as Lars stepped from the stairwell, a gun aimed at Candy's head. "Not here. Let us mourn our father."

Lars rolled his eyes. "Please. You didn't care about that whoring old man any more than I did. Let's go. We've unfinished business. Make it snappy or sweet Candice dies right here."

The tears in Candy's eyes dried and turned to granite. She gave one sniff and marched for the back door. Shar wished she felt as confident as her sister seemed to be. She glanced behind them, hoping for a glimpse of one of her deputies. When she didn't find one, she scuffed the heel of her shoe against the polished vinyl floor. Pretending to drop her keys, she popped a button off her uniform.

"Give me that."

She snapped up. "What?"

"Your radio." Lars held out the hand not holding the gun. "Don't open the door yet, dear Candice, or I shoot your sister."

Just like that, he took away Candy's chance to escape. Shar sighed and handed over her radio. He continued wiggling his fingers until he also had her gun belt, her cell phone, and her pepper spray.

He grinned like a shark, cold and merciless. "Now, we're ready to go." He motioned the gun toward the door.

He marched them to a car hidden in the trees. "Hands behind your backs, chests against the side of the car, please." He zip-tied their hands together, then opened the backdoor and waited for them to get in.

Once he climbed into the driver's seat, he glanced over his shoulder. "All together. Finally. Unfortunately, some of our siblings have disappeared." He widened his eyes. "Did you have anything to do with that, Sharlene?"

"Yes." She refused to be cowed. "Why should I let you torture and kill if I can prevent it?"

"Right. Good little sheriff." He gave a nod and started the ignition. "We don't have far."

Understatement of the year. He took them home. "Will this do?"

"For what?" Shar shifted in her seat. The ties were cutting off the circulation in her hands.

"For our fiery death."

"Not here," Candy said. "This house belonged to our mother."

He stared through the rearview mirror. "Dad's place? That would work, but it might be difficult to get past all those trashy trailers, not to mention dear old Dad wasn't the cleanest person himself." He thought for a moment. "Okay." He steered back to the highway.

A helicopter hovered overhead. Shar closed her eyes and grinned. Neither Everis or her deputies would have let much time pass before using every means necessary to find her. She leaned over and peered out the window. It was definitely a police chopper.

Lars seemed oblivious, even turning the radio to a classical station and drumming along with his fingers on the steering wheel.

Candy nudged Shar with her shoulder, then glanced at the floorboard. "What is it?" she mouthed.

Shar bent over, trying to see what the glint of metal gleaming on the floor was. "I can't tell. Can you get your shoe off? I'll distract—"

"Stop whispering back there," Lars demanded.

"How much time do you have left?" Shar leaned forward, blocking Candy. "I heard you had cancer."

"Considering that I now have the two of you, I'd

say I have maybe an hour." He laughed. "Ain't it grand?" He peered upward through the front windshield. "Ah, it looks as if Mister Agent Man has come for you. Too bad. He should have died back there. I wanted our deaths to be just the three of us."

"Why do you want to kill us? Why the other women?"

He shrugged. "The others were for fun. Their screams—something I made them do—gave me power. Taking their life was the best drug I'd ever taken. My mother was my first kill. She barely whimpered when I stabbed her. After," he held up a finger, "I bashed her head in. Very disappointing." He caught her gaze through the rearview mirror. "As for you and Candice, well, I was denied any siblings in life. I refuse to go through death alone."

"We won't be together, Lars. You're going to hell. You'll spend eternity alone."

"So you say." He stepped on the gas. "Perhaps I should radio your boyfriend and tell him to back off."

"He isn't my boyfriend."

"You're a horrible liar, Sharlene." He directed his attention back to the road. "He's ruining everything." Tires squealed as he took a corner too fast.

Candy yelped and dropped whatever she'd found.

Sharlene slammed against the back driver-side door. "If you aren't more careful, you'll kill us now."

"Hush, sister dear, I need to concentrate." He cut to the left, sending Shar and Candy slamming into the other side door.

"It's a box cutter," Candy whispered. "I had it, but I dropped it."

"Keep trying." Shar pressed her knees against the

back of Lars's seat, doing her best to keep him distracted. An accident was better than being tortured and burned to death.

"Pull over, or we'll fire on the vehicle." Everis's voice came over a loudspeaker.

"I doubt it," Lars said. "They won't shoot with you two in the car."

"I'm a law enforcement officer. He can't hesitate to take you out."

Lars cursed. "Stupid cops." He increased their speed. "How do you ladies feel about a watery death?"

Shar glanced through the front window. The lake loomed ahead, barely visible over the edge of a cliff.

Chapter Twenty-Four

"Oh, God, help us." Shar's gaze fixed on the lake. "Hurry, Candy, or we're going to drown."

Lar's laugh rang out, loud and shrill, manic in its sharpness. "Fire or water, it's all the same to me." He gunned the engine.

"Stop!" Everis shouted over the speaker. The chopper dipped low.

Shar met Everis's frightened gaze through the windshield as the van plummeted over the cliff and plunged front first into the cold waters of Highland Springs Lake. The force of the hit propelled her into the front seat. If not for crouching on the floor searching for the box cutters, Candy would have joined her.

Lars leaned forward against the steering wheel, unconscious. Shar felt for a pulse. Still alive, unfortunately.

Water seeped through any and every crevice. Within seconds, Shar's teeth were chattering. "How are you coming on those cutters? The water is up to the seat."

"I keep dropping it. My fingers are frozen." Candy splashed around her knees.

"I'm going to break the window. If you aren't free by then, kick as hard as you can to the surface. We're sinking further every second." Shar leaned her back against Lars and punched both feet at the window. Nothing. The force of the water kept the glass firmly in place.

She glanced down. "I found a wrench, Candy."

"I've got the cutters. Break that window." Candy reached over the seat and sliced through the ties around Shar's wrist.

Shar hammered at the window with the wrench. A spiderweb of cracks spread across the glass.

"Oh, no, you don't." A hand twisted in her hair, yanking her back.

Shar elbowed backward. "Use the cutters, Candy. Aim for his neck."

Lars pulled a knife from his pocket. By now the water was up to their shoulders. "I'll slit your throat before you get that window open."

Shar slammed her head backward, hearing the satisfying crunch of his nose. She kicked both feet at the window. "Yes." The glass broke free.

Lars cursed.

"Get out, Candy. I've got this." Shar grappled for the knife. "Send help."

Candy shook her head.

"Go!" There was no sense in all of them dying. Just the man trying to stab her.

Candy squeezed past them and out the window. Her foot caught Lars in the chin, snapping his head back and giving Shar an opportunity to gain control. She grabbed his wrists and aimed her knee into his crotch. In the water, she couldn't do much damage, but if she could loosen his grip, it might be enough. The water was up to her chin and rising rapidly. With one final kick to his chest, she took a deep breath and floated out the window.

The surface looked far away—the moon a tiny speck above water a deep indigo. Her lungs burned.

She caught a glimpse of her sister treading water at the surface, and kicked harder. A hand grabbed her ankle, yanking her back.

Lars wrapped his hands around her neck and squeezed.

She flailed out with her feet.

He kept a firm grasp.

Her vision started to fail.

Suddenly, his hand released her. She fought for the surface with her last breath. Her head broke free, and she coughed, gasping for air.

"Shar." Candy wrapped her arms around her. "I thought you were never coming up."

"I was starting to wonder about that myself." The air tasted wonderful, felt cool on her skin. She searched the lake for Lars.

"Everis went down for you."

"What?" Shar whipped back to face her sister.

"He's down there."

No. Shar took several deep breaths and dove under the murky surface. It was too dark to see. Something brushed against her and she kicked with all her being. It did no good. Lars had her hands taught behind her. She gave up and let him pull to the surface.

"What are you thinking?" Everis shook her. "I almost lost, you and you were headed back down?"

"To help you." She caressed his face with her eyes. "Where's Lars?"

"Most likely in hell. His body will surface soon. If not, we'll send down divers."

The light on a small boat shined on them. Minutes later, the three of them were safely aboard and wrapped in warm blankets.

"Sheriff, you sure know how to make a man work for his paycheck." Mayfield grinned and handed her a cup of hot coffee.

"How did you find us?" She glanced at Everis.

"Mayfield found your button. I was searching the woods when he called me. Pinson picked me up, we loaded into a chopper and started searching for you. Pinson is the one who thought Townsend might go back to your place."

She glanced up and met Pinson's gaze. "Thank you."

He shrugged. "He'd want somewhere personal."

"He thought the house was Shar's, but took us away when we told him it was originally our mother's." Candy wrapped both hands around a coffee mug. "We were headed to...our father's trailer when y'all showed up."

Everis sat next to Shar and wrapped his arm around her shoulders, pulling her close.

She leaned her head against him and closed her eyes. "When do you leave?"

"How did you know?"

"The case is done. All that's left is the paperwork."

He sighed. "Three days. I've been reassigned to Phoenix."

She jerked up. "Arizona?"

"Temporary assignment, but I'm not sure how long."

How would she go on without him? In a short time, Everis filled a hole in her heart she hadn't known existed. Candy was right. It really was just the two of them. Men didn't stick around. Whether it was a job or infidelity that took them away, a woman was left alone eventually.

* * *

While Shar didn't seem to have any physical effects from her ordeal, she stayed withdrawn, buried in her work. Everis sat across her desk and studied every line of her face. Not beautiful in the classical sense. Her eyes too light, her nose a bit long, but her lips and the total package couldn't be more perfect.

Arizona seemed a world away. So much for a two-hour relationship.

"Stop staring at me." She looked up and glared.

"Just imprinting."

A smile teased at her lips, but her attention returned to the papers in front of her.

"I'm due a vacation next summer."

"A year."

His shoulders slumped. "I thought maybe I could spend it here with you."

Her eyes pierced his. "In our line of work, we don't know if we'll both still be breathing in a year. What if I'm not sheriff then? What if I move?"

"I'll find you." He reached across the desk.

She hesitated before placing her hand in his. "I hope so." Her eyes shimmered. "I'm going to miss you terribly. You balance me."

"You're the fairest, most compassionate law enforcement officer I've ever dealt with. Your people love you." He wanted to tell her that he loved her, too, but until his future was more solid, he couldn't put that on her. "I need to go, Shar."

Her face fell. "I know."

"I mean, I have to go now." Keeping hold of her hand, he walked around the desk. "But I'm going to kiss you first. I don't want you to forget me."

She gazed up into his face. "As if I could."

He lowered his face and kissed her. The sound of his heart breaking had to be heard into the next county. "I will be back," he whispered against her lips. "I promise."

The End

Stay Tuned for book 2 in The Highland Springs series, "Say Bye to Mommy". Keep reading for an excerpt.

CHAPTER ONE

Ah. She spotted the perfect target. A little girl in a blue dress, the ruffles along the hem torn. Her socks sagging. Dirt marred the chubby legs. Mama browsed the women's clothes, leaving the little one standing in the back of the shopping cart.

The Child Saver as she liked to call herself, quietly stepped up to the cart and pushed it around the corner. "Say goodbye to Mommy." She grinned and continued to the door. It didn't take long for the mother to start shouting her daughter's name. "So, you're Lacey. I think we should call you Lauren to avoid confusion, don't you?" She made her way half-way through the parking lot before the Amber alert sounded.

The Child Saver quickly stashed the little girl in the back of her van and drove away. When the little girl started crying, The Child Saver turned up the radio. Classical music always tamed them. Not as well as a leather strap, but that was at home.

Thirty minutes later, she turned "Lauren" over to Betty to clean up and post her picture on the website, then The Child Saver headed to her job. Not the one that made her money, but the one people thought made her respectable.

She laughed. Right under the good sheriff's nose and no one suspected a thing.

Website at www.cynthiahickey.com

Multi-published and Amazon and ECPA Best-Selling author Cynthia Hickey has sold over a million copies of her works since 2013. She has taught a Continuing Education class at the 2015 American Christian Fiction Writers conference, several small ACFW chapters and RWA chapters. She and her husband run the small press, Winged Publications, which includes some of the CBA's best well-known authors. She lives in Arizona with her husband, one of their seven children, two dogs, one cat, and three box turtles. She has eight grandchildren who keep her busy and tell everyone they know that "Nana is a writer".

Connect with me on FaceBook
Twitter
Amazon
Sign up for my newsletter and receive a free short story
www.cynthiahickey.com

Follow me on Amazon

Enjoy other books by Cynthia Hickey

Shady Acres Mysteries
Beware the Orchids, book 1
Path to Nowhere
Poison Foliage
Poinsettia Madness
Deadly Greenhouse Gases

CYNTHIA HICKEY

Vine Entrapment

CLEAN BUT GRITTY

Colors of Evil Series

Shades of Crimson
Coral Shadows

The Pretty Must Die Series

Ripped in Red, book 1
Pierced in Pink, book 2
Wounded in White, book 3
Worthy, The Complete Story

Lisa Paxton Mystery Series

Eenie Meenie Miny Mo
Jack Be Nimble
Hickory Dickory Dock

Made in the USA
Monee, IL
17 May 2021

68734012R00120